Closer To You

Lauren H. Kelley

LOVESPIN PUBLISHING | ATLANTA

LoveSpin

LOVESPIN PUBLISHING | ATLANTA

This is an original publication of LoveSpin Publishing, LLC.

Published by LoveSpin Publishing
ISBN: 978-0-9898714-3-3

Cover design by LoveSpin Publishing.

Contents

Acknowledgments

To my fabulous editor Yolanda Barber who challenged me every step of the way. To my husband, friends and extended family members who encouraged me to pursue my dream. Thank you all.

CLOSER TO YOU

Second in A Series | A Suits in Pursuit Novel

Lauren H. Kelley

LoveSpin

LOVESPIN PUBLISHING | ATLANTA

CHAPTER ONE

Monday, October 1

The morning came crashing into Kerrigan's senses and her eyes fluttered open. Had last night been a dream? The thought was fleeting as soon as she registered the pain between her legs and deep in her belly. Axel had left her there alone. A million thoughts raced through her mind all at once. The most terrifying of them, he had taken her virginity, and now he would discard her. She tried to move, but every limb ached. Rolling over, she reached for the clock on her nightstand. Ten o'clock. *Shit!* Her manager Marie would be livid.

Then she spotted the small folded piece of paper next to the clock. Nausea came over her as her fingers clumsily opened the note. She released the breath she hadn't realized she held as she began to read.

Good morning sweetheart,

I hope you rested well. Since you didn't sleep much last night, I didn't want to wake you this morning. I'm sorry I couldn't be there when you woke. I have a board meeting this morning. Of course, I'd much rather wake with you. I want you to know how beautiful last night was to me. What we shared, you giving yourself to me and me giving myself to you, changes everything. You've changed my world and opened my eyes to new possibilities. This was an enormous step for us. I don't want you to have any regrets. I don't want you to be afraid of me. I meant every word I said. You're not going to work this week. I want you close to me for a while. I told Brenda that you and I would be out of the office for a few days. Don't panic. She'll get the message to Marie. Remember, I'm still the boss. Marie will be fine. I left something in the kitchen for you. I'll be home by 2:00 p.m. I can't wait to see you.

Only yours,

A

Her heart swelled and the room went blurry, tears clouded her vision. The thought that he could abandon her after last night now seemed silly. She climbed out of bed and went into the kitchen. On the countertop were two-dozen white roses with another note from Axel.

Kerrigan,

Thank you for a wonderful evening. You are the best gift any man could want. These roses are only a small token of my affection for you. I'll be thinking of you until I see you again this afternoon. I have one more surprise for you. Call the number I've written below as soon as you get this.

Only yours,

A

Tears welled up in Kerrigan's eyes, and for a few seconds she couldn't breathe. She caught hold of the countertop to keep herself from wilting to the floor. Only weeks ago, she would have never pegged him as the romantic type, but there she was enraptured by Axel's words, basking in the memory of their lovemaking and night they shared. With shaky hands, she grabbed the phone. Kerrigan barely saw the phone's keypad through her tears, but her jittery fingers managed to dial the numbers left on Axel's note.

A woman answered the phone after it rang a few times.

"Hello," the person on the other end of the call said.

She swallowed hard, and then cleared her throat. "Hi, Um …"

"Is this Kerrigan?" The woman's voice was vaguely familiar to her.

She frowned. "Yes, who's this?"

"Hi, Kerrigan, it's me, Emma. Axel said you'd call. He told me to send a car for you because you'll be staying here for the week."

"Oh! Hi, Emma, I didn't realize … I haven't packed anything. I'll need a little time."

"I have clothes for you dear, and they're already in Axel's closet. You don't need to do anything. He took care of everything for you."

"He did? Is he always like this … so accommodating?"

"No, he's never done anything like this before. I've told you that you mean a lot to him. Whatever is happening between you two, it's the happiest I've ever seen him. He's so calm and relaxed."

"Really?" This was information to process later. "Emma, may I ask you a question?"

"Sure dear. What's on your mind?"

"You said Axel talks about me a lot. How long has he been doing that?"

"He's been talking about you since you showed up at his company. I'll never forget that day. He's all business, all the time, usually. The day he met you though, he came home all chatty. Said he met the most beautiful, intelligent woman. I've known that boy his entire life. He's never done that before."

Kerrigan frowned. Odd, Axel sure confided in his housekeeper an awful lot. "He's never talked to you about his other relationships or other women?"

"What relationships? Before you came along, he rarely dated anyone, and when he did, I never heard anything about any of those women. You can't believe what you read in the papers. He's no playboy. Axel is a good man."

"I guess I'm surprised that he likes someone like me."

"Honey, he's crazy about you. You shouldn't be surprised. Look at you! You're gorgeous, and he's always going on and on about how smart and kind you are."

"Well, thank you. I still don't understand. We're so different in so many ways."

"There's nothing to get. He likes you and you like him. That's all that matters, isn't it?"

"I guess you're right. Thank you Emma. I'll be ready in an hour."

"You're welcome dear. See you soon."

***

An hour later, the car arrived in front of Kerrigan's apartment building. She packed a small bag of essentials and was ready to go when Thomas, the driver, knocked on her door. Knowing she would be at Axel's for the entire week, she had called her mother and brother to let them know she would be away on a work-related trip, which wasn't a complete lie considering he was her boss. She didn't want her family to call out a search party if they couldn't reach her. Luckily, neither of them asked many questions that she wasn't able to answer.

The drive to his house didn't take long. When they reached his estate, it was almost noon. She would have time to settle in and get relaxed before he came home. The car pulled into the driveway, and the grounds were just as beautiful as she remembered. Suddenly, anxiety hit her in the pit of her belly. He'd be home soon, and she'd be there waiting for him, and then what? She wasn't even sure she could look him in the eyes, feeling embarrassed about last night.

She wore blue denim skinny jeans and a teal fitted crop shirt that plunged deeply enough to display her cleavage. She always liked wearing this outfit. Her hair piled on top of her head, loose tendrils framed Kerrigan's face and the nape of her neck. She wanted a reaction from him, but she didn't want to appear as though she was trying too hard.

***

She walked down the familiar hallway from the garage to kitchen. The warm friendly greeting comforted her. "Kerrigan! Welcome dear." Emma briskly wiped her hands on her apron and reached around her, an inviting embrace that soothed her nerves.

"Hi Emma. It's nice to see you again." Releasing her, Kerrigan took two place mats that Emma handed to her. "Thank you again for the pep talk." She glanced over her shoulder at the older woman and gave her a gentle smile as she set the mats on the counter.

Emma winked. "You're welcome dear," then returned to the counter, "Take a seat. Lunch is ready."

Thomas had already taken her small bag upstairs to Axel's bedroom and announced his departure. Emma handed a plate to her and returned to the other side of the island and continued washing and chopping vegetables. Kerrigan didn't have an appetite, even after the rigorous activities of the previous night. Picking through her Waldorf salad, the butterflies in the pit of her stomach returned with a vengeance.

Emma's knife sliced through a tomato. "I'm glad you're here, and Axel is thrilled."

"I'm a little nervous. I don't know why." She fidgeted on the dark wooden stool and popped a carrot into her mouth.

"It's natural dear. Love makes you feel that way." Emma smiled, glancing at her over the rim of the eyeglasses.

Kerrigan frowned. First Ashley and now Emma, too. "L… l … love? It's too soon. I, I don't know," she stuttered, butterflies multiplying in Kerrigan's belly. She hadn't meant, for her voice, to sound so shocked, even though the word love startled her every time she heard it.

"Love isn't restricted by our timelines." Emma placed the knife down and sauntered around the island to the stool next to Kerrigan's. "It was love at first sight when I met my dear Bernie. We met through a mutual friend who set us up on a blind date." Emma stared across the room, a distant memory twinkling in her eyes. "Bernie told me he loved me after only two dates. I felt the same way you do now. I was scared." She swiveled to face Kerrigan. Emma's reassuring gaze was sincere. "He asked me to marry him five days after we met. A few days later, I said yes, and we were married in two weeks." Emma stared at Kerrigan with an intensity that made the hairs on her arm stand on end. "After thirty years of marriage, it's the best decision I ever made, and we're going stronger than ever."

Kerrigan placed her folk down. "That's amazing. What a beautiful story."

The light in Emma's eyes spread to her cheeks as a smile appeared. "Well, I think what's happening between you and Axel is pretty special too." A warm hand patted Kerrigan's arm.

The sting of tears burned behind Kerrigan's eyes. She had been so weepy lately, and she was tired of these emotions. She fought the river building up inside her before speaking again.

"I'm scared, Emma. I've never been in a relationship before. Everything is happening so fast, and I don't want to get hurt. I'm afraid the novelty will wear out, and he'll get bored with me." The dam bursting inside, she blurted out the words before she could stop herself.

"I know my nephew can be demanding. He's always been that way, but he's never been fickle. He's a straight shooter and intensely serious. You're not a fling. He's serious about you."

Kerrigan's eyes nearly bulged out of their sockets. "What? Axel is your nephew!" Her voice pitched, and her brown face turned purple.

"Yes. I live nearby and like to keep myself busy in my old age. He hired me as his part-time housekeeper. I help around the house a few times a week, whenever he needs me. Plus, I get to keep an eye on him." Emma smiled.

"That's great. I hope you'll keep our conversation between us."

Emma stood. "Of course I will. I'm his aunt, but I also know how to respect boundaries. Besides, the two of you have to figure things out for yourselves. Based on everything he's told me about you, I think you're good for him. I think he's good for you too." She patted Kerrigan's hand gently.

As she continued to talk with Emma getting to know her better, her nerves had settled a bit, and she nearly forgot that she was in his kitchen talking with his aunt. She liked Emma. They clicked.

Kerrigan talked about her parents and older brother. Emma told her stories about their family and about him as a boy. "Axel and his brother were always at our house. Bernie and I spent a lot of time looking after Axel and Ryker because my brother and his wife traveled so much. Bernie taught the boys to ride bikes, took them hunting and fishing. When they began dating, he helped them sort through their issues with girls."

"It sounds like you and Bernie had a big influence on him."

Emma nodded her head. "Axel is like a son to me. Bernie and I tried to have a positive influence on him, but of course, he's just like his father. Once his mind is made up about something, there's no stopping him."

Kerrigan could relate. Axel's persistence is what had landed her in his arms.

"When he was about ten years old, he wanted to buy a new bike. Axel was determined to buy the bike by earning his own money. He spent the entire summer with us doing odd chores, and even set up a lemonade stand." Kerrigan smiled at the thought of a younger, enterprising Axel.

"And, I'm just as determined, and still going after what I want," Axel said.

Kerrigan spun around in her seat so fast she nearly got whiplash. Emma startled too, gasping aloud. Glancing up, Kerrigan caught his smoldering look and immediately turned back to her plate. The meaning of his words didn't get lost on her. Those damn butterflies were at war inside her.

"Emma, thank you for everything today," he said.

"Yes, of course. I've got an appointment to get to, so I'm leaving now," Emma announced and winked at Kerrigan as she left the room.

The way he wore the suit, she almost broke into a sweat. He had removed his tie and unfastened two shirt buttons, exposing a hint of his chest. A pool of moisture readied between her thighs. He always had a way of commanding her libido.

Axel didn't say a word. He swaggered over to Kerrigan, swiveled the stool around and positioned himself between her legs. One hand on her waist and the other on her cheek, intense blue eyes stared into hazel ones. Leaning down, his lips covered hers in a deep, passionate kiss. Groaning, he pulled away and helped her down from the stool.

Heartbeat racing and legs trembling beneath her, Axel led them up the stairs, down the hall and to his bedroom. The door slammed. Slowly, he backed Kerrigan up against the back of the door, his hard body pressing into hers. Winded and her legs limp, Axel held Kerrigan close, steadying her.

"Hi, baby," he said in a low, sensual murmur.

"Hi."

"I missed you, so much. I've been thinking about you all day. Let's sit you down. You're trembling."

Taking her hand in his, he led her across the large room and to the bed, covered in a crisp indigo blue and ivory duvet and white linen throw pillows.

"Get off your feet and try to relax, baby." He sat down next to her. "How are you feeling after last night? No regrets. Right?"

The memory of the previous evening still fresh, her cheeks warmed. "I feel good. No regrets."

"Did you enjoy yourself?" His brows pressed together, and he scanned her over.

"You were intense, but the feeling was a good intensity." She offered him a reassuring smile.

He leaned into her, kissing her shoulder and stroking her thigh. "It'll feel better each time we make love. How do you feel about last night?" He muttered the question into the crook of her neck.

She tilted her head, resting her cheek against his forehead. "Last night was perfect. I don't have any regrets." The scorch of his flesh sent tingly waves of shock pulsing through her body.

Straightening himself up, he took one of her hands into his and met her eyes. "Kerrigan, I meant what I said last night, every word."

"I keep thinking ..." She escaped his glare, lips quivering.

"Baby, stop thinking. I'm not about to slow down now. I need you. I want you." He lifted her chin, bringing her eyes back to him.

"Can I ask two stupid questions that have been bothering me?"

"There aren't any stupid questions. What's bothering you?"

"What are we to each other? What's happening between us?" She pulled away and folded her hands in her lap. Her eyes searched his for a guarantee of equal emotion, and her pulse quickened.

"I can answer your second question quite easily. I know we care about each other. My feelings for you are much stronger than you realize, and I think yours are too, although you're afraid to admit your feelings to yourself and to me. You're scared I'll hurt you."

He moved closer to her, his tone softening as he continued. He took her hands into his again. "Your first question is a good one. I'm not into labels. They seem temporary, and I'm not that guy."

"So where does that leave me?" Her voice cracked so badly she gasped for air. "It sounds like your way of not having to make any commitments." Tears pooled in Kerrigan's eyes, the dam ready to burst. He was trying to let her down gently. She had given herself to him, and now he would treat her like nothing more than a friend with benefits. Her heart hammering, palms clammy and stomach turning, she turned her head away. Her eyes landed on the reflection of his legs in the mirrored chest next to his bed.

"That's not at all what I mean," he said, his tone commanding her gaze back to his.

She thought she'd almost seen the corners of his lips pull upward into a smile. She imagined he was pleased with his conquest.

"Last night before we fell asleep, do you remember what I whispered in your ear?"

"No. I was so tired." Her voice revealed a slight tremble.

"Well, I'll have to repeat it then. I'll do a better job this time." He smiled, leaned in closer this time, kissing her lips softly and tenderly.

She was like stone, trying not to cave under the threat of his allure. The way an orchid wilts under the blaze of the hot sun, her resistance was wasted. She surrendered deftly to the inferno of his touch, kissing him back affectionately. She knew all the risks, but she hadn't been able to resist him, even now.

Finally, he broke the kiss. "Kerrigan, how could you think I don't want more with you? What I said last night was that I never want to let you go. It's true—I don't want a girlfriend. I want more. I'm in love with you."

CHAPTER TWO

Axel took her into his arms and consumed her, his tongue invading her mouth as his lips swallowed her cherry flavored ones. Gently lowering her down onto her back, his hand maneuvered underneath her cropped shirt, eager fingers closing the distance between her fleshy round mounds and his firm grasp.

Her nipples hardened. In a swift motion, he raised her shirt above her head and arms, ripping the nuisance away from her body and flinging the rag across the room. Feather light kisses trailed up her stomach until he reached her bosom, and then without warning, he stopped. In a fit of fury, his frantic hands unfastened her teal bra, the lacy garment falling from her arms and landing in her lap.

"You're beautiful. So soft." He delighted in the twist of her right nipple between his index finger and thumb as his lips descended onto her other breast, capturing the tender peak with his delicate nibble.

Pleasure rippled through her body in shocks and waves at the command of his touch. "Ah! Axel."

"I love every inch of your body," he said as he continued his sensual examination of her delicate curves, his hands explored every inch of her.

"I love your body too," she murmured.

His eyes seared her heart. "Touch me, Kerrigan." Raising himself up, he tore his shirt from his flesh.

Her shaky hands reached up, fingers tracing the ridges of his sculpted chest, tickling their way down to the six-pack on his abdomen. His skin blazed in the trail left by her fingertips. He captured her hands with his and anchored them above her head, lowering himself onto her and pressing his lips against hers. Impassioned and at the end of his threshold, he abandoned his seductive hold on her lips, stood and stripped away all barriers between his raw flesh and hers—his dress slacks and gray boxers and her jeans and lace teal thongs landed haphazardly at all four corners of the room. Her breath caught, and eyes stretched wide as they slid down his naked frame, his desire in plain sight. Chest heaving, eyes blinking rapidly and throat swallowing hard, obviously, she hadn't seen his cock in her dimly lit room the night before.

***

Oh, shit! He was enormous. The memory of his cock stretching and filling her still lingered, as did the evidence—her ache. She remembered how hard and deeply he had pounded into her. The feeling of him claiming her had been exquisite, and she wanted him to take her again. With him in full view, panic paralyzed her as she lay stripped and splayed out on the bed motionless, breathless and silent, awaiting his next move.

He stared into her gaze. "Sweetheart, don't be afraid."

She turned her head away, gazing at the clock on his nightstand. "Did, did you fit inside me….completely?" Her words fluttered out.

"Every inch, baby, and I can't wait to be inside you again."

With her eyes shut, she winced. "Axel, please go easy. I'm still sore," she pleaded.

"Baby, I'm sorry I hurt you. I'm about to lose control, so you have to tell me if I'm too rough." The fire in his eyes burned so intensely she melted under the heat.

She nodded her head and gulped the lump in her throat. "Yes, O … Okay." Her voice trembling out the only words she could manage.

She still didn't believe his massive cock had fit inside her. His knees sank into the bed as he climbed in next to her, leaned over and gently stroked her bare legs, making his way up to her golden thighs. His hands found their way between her knees, parting them wide. She was dripping wet for him, soaking with desire. He plunged a finger deep into her as he massaged her clitoris. The intensity surprised her, and she gasped. He inserted another finger, and with an in and out motion, he gently massaged inside her womanhood.

The pleasure inside her built rapidly and she slipped away, feeling nothing but sensation. He removed his fingers and sucked lavishly on them. He kneeled between her legs and pulled her to the edge of the bed. His tongue went to work on her, lapping greedily at the juices of her delicate flower as her delectable honey flowed. He licked and plugged her moist opening with his tongue tasting her tangy, sweet cream.

"Ah. Ah. Axel." She moaned and writhed uncontrollably under his sexual barrage.

He stopped abruptly. "No, not like this. I want you to feel me inside you when you climax."

He immobilized her. She lay helpless in his bed, every inch of her overwhelmed with pleasure, awaiting his next move. He raised himself up and positioned his naked body on top of hers, pushing her legs open as he embedded himself between them. The tip of his shaft sank into her slowly. Inch by inch, his thick, rock-hard cock plunged deep inside her for the second time.

"Ah," she cried as he circled inside her.

She didn't protest, and he wasn't about to stop. With every inch of his throbbing cock thrust inside her, she couldn't help the sounds that escaped her as he filled her and reached her depths. "Oh, god," she yelled out.

"How does this feel?" he asked breathlessly, pumping feverishly into her in rhythmic motion.

She trembled hard underneath him as she submitted her body to his pummeling. "So good," she whimpered.

He slowed his pace to a halt, still inside her. "Kerrigan, I want you to enjoy the feeling of me inside you."

Panting and winded, "I love the feeling of you inside me. My body is yours," she said, clinging on to him tightly.

He lowered his head, sweat glistening on his brow as his lips melded with hers in a slow, sensual kiss. Pulling away, he whispered softly into her ear, "I want your heart too."

Suddenly, his eyes flashed hot and wild, an unnerving intensity. "Last night, I made love to you slow and gentle. Today, I'm not holding back. I'm going to fuck you hard until you beg me to stop."

Oh, shit! The danger in his eyes sent a jolt through her body and her heart hammered in her chest. She gripped his shoulders and her nails planted into his flesh, bracing for his invasion. He slammed into her so hard and deep that all she could do was scream his name repeatedly. He was relentless as he continued pounding into her. Her legs shook uncontrollably as his cock slid in and out, reaching her depths and sending a ripple of vibrations throughout her body so intense that tears formed in her eyes. The feeling that had been an achy soreness subsided and her eyes rolled back, pure sensational ecstasy. Having him inside her, making love to her, fucking her, was the most incredible feeling she had ever had.

She cried out, screaming his name as she climaxed. "Axel, Axel, please. Oh, god."

"I'm not done with you yet," he warned. "I told you before, I want you to beg me to stop."

***

The musky scent of hot sex in the air permeated his senses. Her wavy hair curled tighter, damp and limp as the climate changed in the room from their sweaty bodies merging.

He pulled out of her and lifted himself up. "Baby, get on your knees, lean forward and put your hands on the wall. I want to see your beautiful ass and take you from behind."

The soft gray button-tufted headboard upholstered in velvet banged loudly against the wall, their bodies colliding ferociously. The union of their contrasting skin tones, brown skin to white, tantalized his senses and he slammed into her harder with each blow. Pushing back against his pounding thrusts, she accepted all of him. His hands pinned hers against the wall as he continued ravishing her, pounding into her flesh with full force as he leaned forward and kissed the nape of her neck, inhaling her scent, beautiful feminine heat.

A loud cry escaped her lips, "Please Axel, no more."

He leaned over her, and placed his hand under her chin, tilting her face up to meet his kiss. She moaned into his mouth as her body shuddered all over. He exploded deep inside her, and her walls gripped his shaft hard as she climaxed again for the second, joining him in release.

Exhaling, "Axel," she moaned in a breathy whisper.

He slumped forward, wrapped his arms around her and held her firmly against his glistening chest. "Kerrigan, that was amazing. You're amazing." Slowly, they tumbled down onto the bed in a heap, hot and damp and exhausted. She turned to face him, nestling her head against his chest. "Axel?"

He titled her face to his, searching her eyes. "Yes, baby? You all right?"

"Yes, I'm fine. Um .... I ... I ..." she stammered, pools forming in her eyes.

He knew what she wanted to tell him, but couldn't find the courage to say.

He pulled her closer, caressed her cheek and looked into her eyes. "You don't have to say the words, baby. I know." A smile painted his lips, and he kissed her tenderly on the forehead. "I love you too."

Her lips quivered, tears leaked from her eyes and down Kerrigan's cheeks. He dusted her tear-stained face with tender kisses and held her tight until her tremors calmed. He had never known intimacy like this before. She was afraid to love him, but he was determined to claim her heart, just as he had claimed her body. He couldn't let her go.

He lay there fully sated, silently enjoying her in the afterglow of their passion. He enveloped her small body, folding her in his arms. She was beautiful, radiating with a glow as she slept. He kissed her softly until his eyes fell heavy, succumbing to exhaustion.

***

They spent the next few days together enjoying and learning everything about each other.

She told him about wanting to have her own business one day, a boutique of unique furnishings and eclectic finds. He talked about his plans to take on two new accounts that he hoped would give the company a much bigger share of the market. Every evening ended with passionate lovemaking into the wee hours of the morning.

Early Wednesday morning, he and Kerrigan, went hiking. He knew they shared a love for outdoor activities. Later that afternoon, he took her to a musical festival featuring some of the best local bands. They walked the park grounds hand-in-hand, laughing and enjoying the atmosphere. He noticed strange stares, mostly from older women and a few from younger ones.

He glimpsed down at her and caught her eyes, nervous, unsure, scared. Leaning in, he placed his hand under her soft chin bringing her face to his, "I love you. You're beautiful, smart, kind and sexy as hell. I don't give a damn what anyone else thinks and neither should you. You're my woman, and I'm your man. Say it for me, baby."

Beaming, her eyes sparkled like jewels and her bright smile warmed his heart. Her head placed gently against his chest, she wrapped her arms around him. "Thank you. I'm not easily intimidated, and a few gawkers aren't going to rattle me. You're my man, and I'm your woman."

He kissed her tenderly until her knees wobbled. "We'll finish this tonight."

His cold, hard eyes averted the gawk of the bold onlookers. Whatever their issue was, he didn't care. He clung to her even more, making sure she knew she was his and that she was secure with him.

On Thursday, they went back to his house and lazed around for most of the day. He retreated to his study to work for a few hours while she bathed in the pool and relaxed. He was content to spend a quiet evening at home with Kerrigan. That night, he would test her talents.

Sitting next to her on the sofa in the family room, he shifted his position to face her and asked, "Will you tickle my ivory?"

Her eyebrows shot up, and lips parted.

"I meant play something on the piano for me," he said, as one corner of his mouth slanted into a flirty smile.

She blushed. "I haven't played in years, but I'll try. I love Beethoven's Silence. The piece is beautiful."

He stood. Grabbing her hand, he pulled her to her feet and led her from the casual comfort of the family room into the elegant opulence of his showcase living room. He never liked the space, but his interior decorator talked him into designing a room filled with expensive custom-made furnishings and authentic artwork as a must-have for entertaining.

Kerrigan slinked her way to the ebony Steinway baby grand and sat, fanning out her coral floor-length dress across the black bench. Long, graceful fingers lined the ivory keys, pressing them into melodic symphony as music echoed off the walls filled the room.

Fifteen minutes later, Axel moved from the cream chiffon sofa where he sat, and joined her on the bench, sitting so closely that he saw her chest go from calm to a rapid rise and fall as he closed the distance between them. Her fingers slipped, missing the right notes. The offending sound ended her playing mid-chord.

"If you want me to play, you need to move back. You're making me nervous."

A slow guilty smile perched his lips, and he moved closer until he wrapped his arms around her waist. "You're very talented." He leaned down and kissed her until she panted softly. "Play for me later. I'm going to make love to you, right here and now."

She melted into his touch. "Axel, I…" He shoved his tongue into her mouth, silencing her defense. The clashing sound of random keys being pressed as they leaned against the piano keys impassioned and breathless was their duet.

Releasing her trembling body and with an abrupt move, he turned on the piano's auto-play function. "Shh, baby. Don't say a word. Let me make love to you." A soft melody filled the room once more.

The second he resumed his touch, caressing and fondling her, she was his again, lost in the sensual heat of his command. "Yes," she whispered a raspy reply.

Entwined and enraptured with Kerrigan, he slipped to the floor bringing her hot, writhing body onto his. He made love to her there on the floor, on the sofa and on the piano, tenderly, all night.

The memory they made that night would forever change his opinion of the stodgy room.

CHAPTER THREE

Friday, October 5

Early Friday morning Axel and Kerrigan drove two hours north to spend the weekend at his mountain cabin. He didn't immediately tell her where he was taking her. Half way to their destination, he broke the news.

He glanced at her cautiously. "Are you sure you want to know where we're heading?" Suddenly, his stomach was heavy, like stones resting inside.

Her head leaned back against the black leather headrest. She turned away from the scenic view of magnificent pines and caught his glare. "Yes! Axel, stop teasing me and tell me where we're going."

The cool breeze coming in from the open window calmed his nerves. "Okay. Okay. We're going to spend the weekend at my cabin. It's near a quaint little town in the north Georgia Mountains." The right indicator light blinked as he switched lanes getting behind a blue minivan. Better to be in the slow lane for this conversation.

"Sounds lovely." She turned toward the road and closed her eyes.

He cleared his throat. "I've made sure we get to spend time together on Saturday evening." His white-knuckled grip on the steering wheel helped him brace for impact.

Her eyes sprang open, and she jerked forward as she turned to face him, harnessed by the seat belt pressed against her pastel pink shirt between her breasts. "Only on Saturday night? What does that mean? Is there something you're not telling me?" Her voice pitched.

"Well … tonight Ryker and mom and dad are joining us at the cabin. And tomorrow, the guys are going fishing ..." He paused, and then glanced at her, watching her expression.

Her mouth fell open. "What! You didn't tell me that I was going to meet your family." She placed her hand on her forehead. "Things are moving too quickly," she muttered under her breath and shook her head. "I'm not ready to meet them yet. I didn't pack appropriately. Do they know anything about me?" She rattled off, her voice raising several octaves.

Shifting in his seat, he stiffened. "Yesterday, I told mom that you'd be coming. They've known about you for a while." He cleared his throat again. "I may have mentioned you a few times." He couldn't help the guilty grin that spread across his face. "Don't worry about your clothes. You always look gorgeous."

She stared at him with narrowed eyes, scowling. "I can't believe you. Meeting your parents isn't something you can just spring on me at the last possible minute. What do they think about your dating a black woman?" He could see the worry on her face, her forehead wrinkling the way it did when she was frustrated or upset about something.

Lips pressed together, he regarded her with a gentle touch to her arm now folded across her chest. "I've never mentioned your race to my family. It doesn't matter. Kerrigan, you're not some strange three-headed alien. You're a human being, and I love you. The color of our skin shouldn't make a difference. Besides, I happen to think that our contrasting skin tones are visually stunning when we make love."

A subtle shade of rouge tinted her cheeks at his remark, but it didn't deter her irritation. "Axel, you can't make light of this. You and I might not have any issues with our differences, but some people might. I'm not accusing your parents of being racists, but prejudice is alive. I am acutely aware of that fact every day. The color of my skin shouldn't matter, but sometimes it does. What do your parents think about interracial relationships?" Her frigid tone and glossy-eyed stare hit him in the gut like a sack of potatoes.

Quiet for a moment, he thought about the position he would be putting her in.

He reached over and grabbed her hand. "Baby, I'm sorry. I understand how you feel. I wish I could take away your pain." He regarded her with a half smile. "I've never talked with my parents about interracial dating or relationships, and I honestly don't know what they'll think, but they raised me to treat all people with dignity and respect, regardless of race, gender or social status." He glanced at her trying to gauge her reaction. She was an ice cube, motionless and staring at the winding, tree-lined road ahead.

He pulled his hand away, needing both of them on the steering wheel as the vehicle swerved over onto the shoulder and came to an abrupt stop.

She gasped. Her eyebrows pressed together in a V, and the harsh intensity in her eyes faded, her expression softening into a perplexed daze.

Cars, trucks, SUVs and eighteen-wheelers passed by them in loud swooshes. The parked vehicle shook. His fingers reached out and glided, from her temple, and then to her chin. He leaned over, pulled her closer, pecking her softly on the lips and then peeled away. "I don't give a damn if anyone has an issue with us, including our families. I want you to meet my family." He reclaimed his hold on her hand. "Kerrigan, you're important to me, and I want my family to know how much you mean. I hope to meet your family one day soon, too. What will they think?" He gave her hand a light squeeze.

"My family is so diverse they wouldn't even think twice about us. They'd mostly care that we're happy." She paused, nervous eyes looking up to his. "I don't know about this, but I suppose I have no choice do I?" Her eyes filled with moisture, ready to flow.

He squeezed her hand tighter. "Sweetheart, I'm sorry for springing this on you. I didn't think this through, how you might feel about meeting my parents." He kissed her again, softly. "I don't think about us in terms of color. I'm just a man and you're the woman I love. I wish you weren't so concerned about what others think."

She turned her head away. A single tear trickled down her cheek. "Right or wrong, what others think does matter to me," she said mumbling under her breath.

***

Kerrigan tensed as she thought about meeting Axel's parents. Although a success in his own right, he came from money. She was certain that his parents had different plans for their son that probably didn't include him falling in love with someone like her. She remained silent the rest of the trip. What type of woman, would Mrs. Christensen be? If she were anything like Emma, perhaps she and Kerrigan would get along well.

The SUV turned down the long twisting driveway. As the secluded log cabin came into view, she saw two other vehicles parked in front of a double car garage. Her heart raced. His family was already there. The trepidation that had been building inside her came bubbling to the surface. She didn't utter a word. The vehicle came to a halt as the engine idled behind a silver Lexus sedan. Leaning toward her, he took one of her hands in his, the palm of his other hand caressing her cheek softly. She leaned into his touch.

"Sweetheart, I'm really sorry for doing this to you, but I promise there's nothing to worry about. I won't let anyone hurt you. Kerrigan, I'm in love with you. You're afraid to admit your feelings, but I know you feel the same about me. I see the way you look at me, even now, the way you respond to my touch, and your spoken and unspoken words. I want more with you, so much more and I think you do to, and I want both our families to know about us. If I'm wrong, tell me now, and I'll turn around, and we can go back to the city." He shifted away from her and rubbed his chin.

She closed her eyes and breathed in the clean mountain air that drifted in through the open sunroof. "You're not wrong," she whispered softly.

A sexy crooked smile perched on his lips. "We'll have a terrific weekend. Just try to relax."

His smoldering gaze and his sensual touch turned her to mush. He captured her trembling lips with his. His kiss, slow and deep until she melted into him, was sweet seduction. His hand covered her breast. He would have made his way under her eyelet shirt if not for the sudden loud banging that came from the driver side window. She jolted back slamming into the passenger door and gasped. Turned in his seat, he rolled his eyes as he slid his hand to the door and pressed a button to roll down the window.

"What the hell, bro? I'm a little busy here with my lady or hadn't you noticed?" He regarded the man standing outside the vehicle with a stern, but playful look.

Ryker was a few years his junior. His dark tousled hair, tall wiry frame and olive colored skin resembled Axel's, except Axel's build was hulking and muscular. Eyes, a less intense shade of blue, stared back at her. The man's handsome face was a younger version of his brother's, but boy-like.

Axel's brother smirked with the same devious visage that she had come to know all too well. "I was trying to rescue her from you," he returned, sticking his head through the window. He passed Axel and regarded her directly. "Kerrigan, I'm sorry my brother has such poor manners. You'll have to forgive him. Are you okay?" She laughed. She knew she would like Axel's brother already. "I can contain him if he gets out of hand again," Ryker said and then smiled.

"Thank you, Ryker. That's kind of you, but I know I'm in good hands with your brother."

Axel turned back to her, smiled and squeezed her hand. "That you are." He leaned close to her so only she could hear his next words. "I'll show you later just how good my hands are," he said in a seductive growl. "Come on. I want you to meet the rest of the family. They're not as ornery."

Axel exited the black SUV, and jogged around to her side, opened the door and helped her down. Protectively, he put his arm around her petite waist and held her close to him. Walking toward the cabin, Kerrigan halted her steps, planting her feet firmly on the cobblestone path as she took in the looming forest, echoes of life teaming around her and rays of sunlight that singed her skin as beams filtered down through the scattered branches above. Ryker had gone ahead of them, shoving their bags through the cabin door.

Axel tilted his head, his forehead wrinkling. She knew that expression. "I'm fine," she said, placing her arm around his waist as she leaned against him. "The air is so fresh, and the sunshine feels good. The mountains are so beautiful." Inhaling, earthy moss filled her nostrils.

He tightened his hold on her, and then kissed her forehead. "Are you sure you're not just stalling?" Tugging her forward, he coaxed her feet to move again, small twigs and pine needles crunching under Kerrigan's steps.

"I'm nervous." She glanced up at him, and then nuzzled her head against his chest. "Okay, maybe I'm stalling a little." She conceded.

They reached the front door. He gave her behind a light squeeze. "Ah! Axel!" she squealed.

"Baby, I promise, everything is going to be fine. Let's go inside."

As they entered the foyer, she heard a man's voice and the faint sound of a woman's laughter coming from the family room. The knot that formed in her stomach twisted. He pulled her closer as they made their way into the rustic room. Earth tone colors and shiplap-covered walls was just what she imagined. On either side of a fireplace, two large windows ran along the back of the house and ran the height of the two-story room, letting in bright streams of light, and a breathtaking view of the lakefront.

His mother, a willowy woman with long dark hair, sat on a brown leather sofa next to her husband. She was a beauty in her own right. The second they entered the room, Axel's mother jumped out of her seat and made her way over to them. She reached out her arms to Axel. He pried himself away from Kerrigan as she took him into her warm embrace. She studied his face carefully before speaking.

"Son, you look well, relaxed even. I haven't seen you look so at peace in the longest time. It makes my heart happy." She smiled before turning to regard Kerrigan. "And this must be the young woman I have to thank for your bright disposition. It's a pleasure to meet you, Kerrigan. I've heard your name for months now. I'm Elizabeth."

Kerrigan had prepared herself for a formal handshake. Instead, she was greeted by a tight hug that loosened the tangle in her belly. "It's nice to meet you too."

After releasing Kerrigan, Elizabeth turned back to Axel.

"You've had a long drive." She smiled. "Come on in and take a seat."

"Thanks. We are tired," he said, grabbing Kerrigan's hand and leading her into the large room.

Axel's father, who had been reading, peered over the top of the book in his freckled hands, and with a nod, he regarded his son. Axel was a carbon copy of his father, who had thirty or so years on his son and was more refined with a full head of salt-and-pepper-colored hair that gave him a distinguished air.

His eyes shifted to her and then back to him. He studied the pair for a moment before speaking.

"I don't know how you managed to snare such a beautiful woman son." He stood to greet them as they made their way toward him.

He placed the book on the edge of a side table. "Hi, Kerrigan, I'm John." Axel's father wrapped her in his arms, patted her on the back, and then studied her from arms length.

"I hope my son is treating you well." Now she knew where Axel's smile came from.

She smiled back. "Yes sir, he's a perfect gentleman." Her earlier worries were wasted.

CHAPTER FOUR

Kerrigan sat on the oversized leather sofa, and Axel followed, sitting next to her and extended his arm around her shoulders, snuggling her close. Elizabeth and John returned to the smaller love seat.

"Kerrigan, you must know this is the first time that Axel has ever introduced us to a girlfriend," Elizabeth beamed.

She peeked up at Axel with curious hazel eyes and smiled brightly. He loved the way her face lit up and how her smile reached her eyes. He raised his brow, and then nuzzled his cheek against her temple.

Giving Kerrigan's shoulder a squeeze, Axel turned his head toward his mother's tender smile. "I told you that she's extremely special to me. I wouldn't waste time introducing her to you if she weren't."

"Sounds as if we'll be seeing a lot more of you dear," John said, giving her a wink.

"How did the two of you meet?" Elizabeth asked.

"Mom, Kerrigan came to work for A. C. Advertising little over a year ago. Besides being a stunning beauty, she has a brilliant marketing mind. I was crazy about her the moment she stepped foot into my office." With a slight nod of his head, he gave his father a knowing look, eyebrows raised.

"That's right." John tapped his index finger against his chin. "Didn't you call me the day you met her? I remember now. Axel was enamored with you instantly. He called me to say that he had met the most incredible woman." John lowered his hand to his lap and fixed his eyes on Kerrigan.

Kerrigan stared at Axel, mouth agape. He had never disclosed that information to her before.

"Kerrigan, did you feel the same instant attraction to Axel?" Elizabeth asked.

"I don't think she did." He answered for her, wanting to spare her from his parent's inquisition.

"Let Kerrigan answer for herself," his father piped in.

"Yes, I felt an immediate attraction to him, but I never thought seriously about Axel. I didn't think he would be interested in me," she replied timidly.

Axel raised his brow. Her news surprised him. "Hmm. I think you know just how interested I am now," he whispered into her ear.

She blushed, and swiped her hand at him playfully. "I pursued her until she gave in. You know how relentless I can be when I set my sights on something I want." Axel flashed a deliberately wicked smile at Kerrigan.

Lifting his arm from around her, he rested his forearms on his thighs and leaned forward, addressing his parents with narrowed eyes glaring. "That's enough with the interrogation. How are things at home? Dad, are you working on any interesting cases?"

He hoped the diversion tactic would work.

***

Ryker had been in and out of the cabin, taking their luggage to the room, which should have only taken him two trips. He still had not joined them in the family room. His parents talked about the latest gossip in his their hometown. Dad told them about a couple of his more intriguing cases. Mom shared stories about her squabbles with some of the women from their neighborhood association's event committee. He sat and pretended to listen, but what he wanted was to be alone with her.

After a half an hour of conversation, he rose and held his hand out to Kerrigan to help her up from the sofa. "Mom, dad, if you'll excuse us, we're going upstairs to unpack, rest and freshen up for the evening. We'll be back down later."

As they made their way out of the room, his father spoke out.

"Son, can I see you for a brief moment in private?"

He nodded at her, signaling for Kerrigan to go upstairs without him. "We're the last door on the right," he called out to her. "I'll be right up."

"Okay." She smiled at both men and darted up the stairs, heading toward the room.

He walked over to his dad, who stood in front of the large window peering at the lake. Mom had retreated to the kitchen. Father and son were alone.

"Son, she's beautiful, but I want you to be careful. Are you using protection? I'm not saying I think anything ill of Kerrigan, but I hear horrendous stories every day, and I encounter much of the litigation. Remember to be careful about sex. You don't know her entire history."

He jerked his head back, nostrils flaring.

Adjusting his stance, he planted his feet wide apart, and shoved his hands into the pockets of his khaki cargo pants. "Dad, I appreciate your concern, but I'm thirty-three years old. I don't have to worry about much. Her history, as you put it, started with me." He glared coldly at his father and then glanced out the window at the serene lake.

John's mouth opened forming a circle, "Oh?" His eyes swelled, bewildered. "Has she only been with you? Are you sure?" The tone of his voice reached new heights.

Axel's lips flattened as he withdrew his hands from his pants pockets. "Yes, I'm quite positive she was a virgin when we met. I'm curious." He paced from the bottom of the staircase and glanced up, and then back to where John stood at the window. "Why are you being negative? Does your concern have anything to do with her race?" He folded his arms across his chest defensively, his body tense and temperature beginning to rise.

John stepped forward and reached his thin hand out to Axel's chest. "I'm not being negative, and of course my concern has nothing to do with her race." Axel stepped back, yanking his left shoulder away from John's reach. "Son, she's the first woman you've ever brought home. I suppose I've always wanted to have this conversation with both you and Ryker, but there was never a reason. Neither of you seemed to be serious enough about a woman to bring her home." He stepped forward toward Axel. "I see the way you two look at each other. You're a wealthy young man. A cunning woman can do things to trap you or take your money if you're not careful. You know what I mean. Think of what happened with Sara."

Axel's jaw clenched shut. "Sara is precisely the reason I haven't been able to have a healthy relationship." His temper building, his tone escalated. "I was traumatized by that ordeal. I intentionally dated women I knew I could never get serious about, but Kerrigan has changed all that." He bared his teeth at his father, an acid grin. "She's financially secure, all on her own merit. She's not after my money and I can't think of anything she could do to trap me, so why don't you elaborate?" His temperature soared.

Leathery fingers curled over Axel's shoulder. "Son, I'm talking about pregnancy. I'm an attorney. I have a different perspective based on the things I've seen and experienced over the years."

He backed away from John's anchoring hand again. "What I share with Kerrigan is much more than superficial. I want more with her than a casual affair. If I were to get her pregnant, it wouldn't be the worst thing in the world." Axel cracked his knuckles, and his heart pounded in his chest.

John's tone softened. "Son, just be careful."

He gritted his teeth, "Not that my relationship is any of your business, but I've been the one in pursuit." He couldn't believe his father's gall. "She's the only woman I've ever met who hasn't offered herself up on a platter to me or tried to dig into my pockets. She's been hesitant and apprehensive, afraid I will hurt her. She's a genuinely good person with a beautiful heart. I'm in love with her so you'd better get used to the idea." If he didn't end the conversation soon, he would say or do something he'd later regret. "Now if you'll excuse me ..." He whipped around and headed toward the staircase.

"Axel, I'm glad you're happy." John yelled after him, drawing Axel's attention as he turned to face him. "You've become a good judge of character, and I know you're an adult, but I wouldn't be a good father if I didn't express my concern. Maybe one day you'll know what being a parent is like."

Their conversation ended, and Axel bounded up the stairs, taking two at a time, his pulse racing as he fumed.

CHAPTER FIVE

Axel entered the room. Unusually tired that afternoon, though understandable given the events of the day, Kerrigan slept. She was always radiant, even in slumber and her beauty a calming force. He eased onto the bed next to her, studying her delicate caramel-colored features and admiring her beauty, relishing the curve of her full soft lips that he longed to kiss. He wanted to have some intimate time with her, but the events of the afternoon had been a bit much for him too. He lay down and curled himself around her. She nestled her body into his, their fit snug like a glove on a hand. They slept soundly for hours.

***

When Kerrigan awoke, the time was four fifteen in the afternoon.

Axel greeted her with his handsome face. "Hey sleepy head, why don't we go join the family downstairs? I'm sure Ryker must be going out of his mind alone with those two."

She squirmed, still feeling a little tired. "Okay. Let me freshen up first."

He flashed a devilish grin at her. "I'll join you."

They entered the bathroom together. She walked ahead of him while he playfully tugged at her shirt until he had wrapped his arms around her waist. Not elaborately decorated like the ones in his house, she noted that the bathroom was still large and impressive. The style was rustic, like the rest of the cabin, earth tones and wood-covered finishings. They stood in front of the mirror looking at their reflection. She rested her head back against his smooth chest and closed her eyes. She felt safe in those arms, the irony that nothing in the world could hurt her except him.

He slipped his hands into the sides of her pants and slid the tight jeans down slowly until they pooled around her ankles onto the floor. He reached around her, unbuttoned her eyelet shirt and let the garment fall to the ground. There she stood in a pink lace bra and matching panties. He strode to the Jacuzzi and filled the tub with piping hot water. His attention turned to her again, and he made his way back to where she stood. Lifting his shirt over his head, he tossed the material aside. She salivated at the sight of his sexy chiseled body. He unzipped his pants, his erection pressing against the fabric of his boxer briefs. Stepping out of the pants, he kicked them aside.

With his bare hands, he ripped her lacy panties to shreds and hoisted her onto the edge of countertop, and spread her legs wide and he stood between them. The musky smell of his masculinity invaded her senses and moistening, she readied for his sensuous touch. He unfastened her bra, freeing her perky breasts. His sheathed rod pressed firmly against the delicate folds of her moist opening. He pulled down his boxer briefs and his cock plummeted out. Without hesitation, he gripped his shaft and guided himself into her, entering her slowly as she adjusted to his size. She gasped at the intensity of him filling her. She clutched his shoulders as he pumped into her hard. Her back arched as the intensity of their lovemaking heightened. Her breasts bounced freely up and down with each of his powerful thrusts.

He pounded into her so hard that she couldn't help the scream that escaped her lips. A hand flew up to cover her month.

"Let go, baby. Scream for me, as loudly as you want. No one can hear you, only me."

She hoped he was right. The loud sound of the Jacuzzi's jets roaring and insulated walls would drown out her cries. He pummeled her hard now, her body convulsing in sheer pleasure as every nerve ending fired in response to his thrusts.

"Axel. Axel." She cried loudly.

"That's it, baby. I love the way you moan my name."

They exploded together, she around his hard shaft and he deep inside her.

"You feel so good, Kerrigan."

She leaned forward and placed her head onto his sculpted chest. His arms wrapped tightly around her and his warm naked body pressed against hers made her head spin.

His swollen erection was still inside her. Without caution, strong arms lifted her off the counter and he stepped into the middle of the bathroom.

"Can you handle round two?" he asked, sweat pouring down his face.

Her arms wrapped tightly around his thick neck, and her legs spanned his waist. "Yes," her soft whisper tickled his ear.

He gripped her thighs firmly, raised her up and impaled her with his hard shaft. Repeating the motion, he penetrated her fully.

"Ah. Ah. Oh, god." The delicious moan escaped her lips until the pleasure built to the apex once more, rendering her silent.

"Fuck," he groaned loudly, sliding her up and down on his slick cock.

Trembling all over, she found her release again. Limbs limp like wet spaghetti, she clung to him for strength. Thrusting into her with full force, a loud cry, emerged from her depths, another instantaneous release. "Ah. Axel. Axel."

His load spilled into her for a second time before he gently placed her back onto the countertop.

He leaned in, capturing her soft full lips with his and kissed her slowly. "Kerrigan, you have no idea what you do to me. I can't get enough of you," he panted.

Her hands still trembled, but she maintained a tight grip on his shoulders. "Me too," she replied breathlessly.

"Come on. Let's bathe and head downstairs or I'm afraid they'll never see us again," he teased.

Helping her down from the cool countertop and he led her by the hand to the tub filled with steaming water. Kerrigan stepped in first and seated herself. Axel entered and sat behind her. She could feel his cock rising, pressing against her behind.

"I told you that I couldn't get enough of you," he whispered.

"You'll have to save it for later. Weren't we supposed to be downstairs thirty minutes ago?"

"I don't care. I want time alone with you. Turn around, face me and ride, baby."

She eagerly complied, guiding herself gingerly onto his shaft. His fingers sank into her thighs, his grip bringing her down onto his cock.

"Kerrigan, I want to savor you. Don't move, be still."

Deep inside her, Axel gently rocked her back and forth. The water surged around them, crashing into the tub's sides, nearly overflowing and splashing to the floor, their swaying movement the cause. He ground deeply inside her, almost in slow motion.

She shuddered all over. Gasping, "Ah. Ah," she released soft cries into his ear.

Tenderly, he held her close to him, face-to-face, searing blue eyes ablaze and sensual, searched hers. He whispered in her ear. "You're mine, always. Say it for me, Kerrigan."

His thickness slipped in and out of her, warm and sinewy, pressing, reaching the depths of her desire. Her eyes rolled back and she moaned a breathy response. "I … I'm yours … always."

In this position, her orgasm had been prolonged, moments fading into minutes. She had never felt anything like this before. Tears leaked, trickled down her cheeks and splashed onto his shoulder, down his chest. He searched her eyes again. Her tears were an emotional release, a sensation he experienced with equal weight. He crushed her lips with his, capturing her sweet sobs. He held her tightly and continued the slow rocking motion until the full intensity of the wave of pleasure had passed. When their lovemaking had ended, she shuddered uncontrollably, every part of her weak.

He had worked her over good. Neither of them had experienced an intimacy so extraordinary. It was pure emotion and unbridled ecstasy. She barely could stand, and she was more tired than before their earlier nap. He helped her bathe and ordered her to lie down. Kneeling, he planted a soft kiss sweetly on her forehead.

"Mmm," she whimpered softly at his touch.

His eyes met hers, tender and tired. "I love you, Kerrigan. You belong to me, always," he whispered as she closed her lids and drifted to sleep.

***

Renewed and invigorated, Axel bounded out of the room and headed down to the family room. His parents weren't there, but when he entered, he was greeted by a round of applause from Ryker who was stretched out across the sofa. "Way to go big bro. You gave it to her good, didn't you? You were up there for hours."

"Can you at least pretend to be somewhat civilized? We napped. She's still asleep, and I didn't want to wake her," he moved to the chair next to the sofa and fell into it.

"Right," Ryker said, his tone cynical. "A woman as hot as Kerrigan is lying in your bed, and you expect me to believe you didn't fuck her senseless."

"You're an immature ass. It's no wonder you're single. What I do with my woman, in my bedroom, in my cabin is none of your business." He placed his feet up on the ottoman, getting comfortable.

Ryker sat upright and faced Axel. "It is my business when everyone in the cabin can hear you two."

"What! You heard us?" He gripped the front end of the chair's arm, digging his nails into its leather, and leaning forward.

"Yep, and so did mom and dad. They couldn't take it anymore. They went out to dinner."

Axel grimaced. "I didn't think anyone would hear us. I had the Jacuzzi jets on. Don't say anything to her. She'll be mortified."

Ryker grabbed a fishing magazine from the table next to the sofa and pulled it up, covering his devious smile. "I'm just messing with you. No one heard a thing, but I knew you weren't just napping up there."

"You're so juvenile. Grow up!" The tension in Axel's face loosened.

Ryker flipped the pages of the magazine haphazardly. "So what's it like with her? She's one impressive piece of tail." His eyes peered over the magazine into Axel's glare.

Axel lowered his bare feet from the leather ottoman, placed his forearms on his knees and leaned in. "Ryker, I'm going to say this one more time." He spoke with clipped words beneath gritted teeth like a master ventriloquist. "Kerrigan is my woman. She's not a piece of tail. If you talk about her in a disrespectful or disparaging way again, I'll pulverize your face and kick you out on your ass." Jeering at him, the pitch of his voice deepened, words meant to sound harsh and firm.

"So, you're serious about her? My apologies, I didn't mean to offend."

"I am serious about her. I'm in love with her."

Ryker lifted his eyes up from the magazine and eyed him speculatively. "Wow. Really?" His brows arched and mouth fell open. "I never thought I'd see the day. The mighty and powerful Axel Christensen succumbs to a woman, to little Kerrigan Mulls no less," he said.

Running his fingers along the chairs slick arm, Axel leaned back into the chair. "She's the one."

Ryker tossed the magazine onto the wooden side table, his eyebrows shooting up in shock. "The one, huh? Does she know?"

"She knows how I feel about her—that I love her. I haven't said anything more than that, yet." Axel stared out the window watching the sun sink into the lake as it began to set. The sunset paralleled his life—the ending of one day and the anticipation of the next, filled with new mysteries, to be uncovered.

"More?" Ryker's question brought his focus back. "You mean marriage?"

Axel twisted around and set his determined eyes on his brother. "Yes, when the time is right. Now, stop grilling me. What about you? Is there anyone significant in your life?"

"No. I'm still enjoying the single life. If I had someone like Kerrigan, I might be persuaded to settle down, too." Ryker winked.

He stood and moved to the large window, and then turned to face Ryker. "Someday, I'm sure you'll find the right woman."

He knew what he wanted—what he felt for her. This was the very reason that he wanted her to meet his family, but the thought that he was ready to settle down was still fresh. Although he was nervous, he was not a man to run away from his feelings. Instead, he embraced them fully. Standing at the window, he formulated his next move. He had to tear down her walls completely.

CHAPTER SIX

Saturday, October 6

At the dawn of the next day Axel, his dad and Ryker went fishing on the lake, leaving Kerrigan and his mother alone to bond. The men sat at the end of the dock baiting and casting their lines as steam rose off the murky water and the smell of peat algae filled the air. Ryker had been acting strangely, barely talking and eyes shifty. Axel suspected Ryker was up to something.

"Dad, did you know that Axel is planning to ask Kerrigan to marry him?" Ryker stuck his hook through a thick black worm, sneering at Axel while his legs dangled off the edge of the dock.

His line sunk into the water, John pivoted and pinned Axel with his gaze. "Son, is this true? Have the two of you discussed marriage?" Silence fell between them. The only sound that could be heard was the gentle lap of water slapping the dock.

Axel shot Ryker a fiery look, and then turned to face his father. "No, dad, we haven't discussed marriage yet. I haven't decided when I'll ask her, but I do intend to propose soon." He tilted his white cap, masking his face from the burning rays of morning sunlight.

A tug on his line forced John's focus back to the water. "What about her family. Have you met them?" John asked over his shoulder, competing with the sputter of a boat motor off in the distance.

With a quarter turn and throw of his shoulder, Axel cast his line into the lake. "Nope. I know all about them though. Her mother is a retired teacher." The hiss of Ryker's beer can opening stole his gaze. "She teaches piano lessons and tutors children. Her father worked in law enforcement—semi retired. She has an older brother who's married and has a set of twins. He's a cardiovascular surgeon."

John nodded. "Sounds as if she comes from a decent stock of people," he said. Winding the reel his arms flailed, and he struggled with his catch.

Axel's eyes burned hotly. "What the hell is that supposed to mean?" His voice pitched.

Pressing his lips together, "I'm just saying that her family sounds as if they're decent people," John said, glancing at Axel, his forehead wrinkled.

Axel adjusted the lid of his cap, staring across the lake and not making eye contact. "You mean because she's, not from a family of elites and Ivy Leaguers or because she's black?" Axel tilted his head from left to right, loosening his neck.

Sounds of the surrounding forest coming to life could be heard all around them, birds chirping, frogs croaking, and insects buzzing as the crispness of the early morning faded into sweltering humidity under the sun.

John's shoulders stiffened, and his face turned a shade of red that matched the t-shirt he wore. "Axel, you're twisting my words. That isn't what I said." His rod slammed into the dock planks with a loud thud. "Shit! I lost the damn thing."

Axel wound his line. "No, that isn't what you said, but isn't that what you meant? I suggest that you get over any issues you have with Kerrigan. She's in my life, to stay." The tone of his voice rose.

Axel glared at Ryker, who sat back, a smug grin resting on his lips enjoying the spat while he pulled and tugged, struggling with the fish at the end of his line.

"Son, I don't have any problems with you two or Kerrigan, or her family. I really do like her. You're being overly sensitive. She makes you happy and I want that for you." John placed another worm onto his hook. "I think your mother will be thrilled to help plan a wedding." Slimy palms slid across John's lap, wiping residue onto his jeans.

Axel calmed and observed at his dad pensively, eyes narrow and lips pursed. "I'm in defense mode when it comes to Kerrigan. She's sensitive about how others perceive our relationship." He exhaled a deep breath and his posture slumped.

John sat his rod down and turned to Axel. "Son, my reaction is simply out of concern for you, especially after everything you've gone through with Sara. I guess I'm still wounded as I know you are." He stared at Ryker, nodded his head disapprovingly, and then shifted his eyes back to Axel. "A word of advice for the health of your relationship—you both need to get a handle on your insecurities. A relationship takes hard work, and you're bound to have critics. The important thing to remember is that you get out of life what you expect, whether it's real or manufactured in your mind. If you love each other, then that's what matters." John dropped his line again, lips pressed into a thin line and eyes squinting, the grit of determination riddled across his face. "Son, my concern was for you and not about Kerrigan or anything else."

His heart rate back to normal, Axel nodded his head. "I'm sorry, dad. I know you're only looking out for me." Eager fingers clawed, through the ice chest, to grab a beer. Axel appreciated his father's words and knew his father was right about one thing—the insecurities in their relationship had to be addressed.

Ryker held his head down and leisurely lifted his eyes to meet Axel's leer. He mouthed, "Sorry, bro."

A slow roll of his eyes back at Ryker, Axel huffed. "It's all good. Gentlemen, we have some fishing to do. Let's get to it."

Yanking his line from the water, John pulled out the large trout that lost its struggle against the line.

"Now, that's a thing of beauty." John piped up and flashed his pearly whites.

Ryker stretched his hand out. "Hey, pass me that bucket," he demanded, his competitive nature awakened. "I'm going to catch the prize fish today."

John let out a hearty laugh. Axel shoved the bucket to his brother. "We'll see."

The three men continued fishing, the tension finally dissipating into vapors like the steam rising from the lake into the mid-morning dank.

***

Inside the cabin, Kerrigan and Elizabeth lounged, the salty sweetness of kettle corn wafting as they watched The Notebook. She liked Elizabeth, who seemed like a sweet woman, but Kerrigan braced for an onslaught of questions.

Elizabeth's graceful fingers, pale and expertly manicured, waltzed across the wooden trunk that served as a cocktail table. She grabbed hold of the tablet-styled, touch screen remote control. Jabbing the pause button, she brought the movie to an abrupt halt. "Are you in love with my son?" she blurted out.

Kerrigan's eyes shifted from the flat screen and darted to Elizabeth. Her pulse went from a calm resting rate to 175 beats in an instant.

Pulling the plaid tapestry throw around her shoulders tight, she gnawed mercilessly at her bottom lip. "Honestly, that's a difficult question for me to answer. This is new territory for me—the first relationship I've ever had." Kerrigan crossed her arms over her stomach.

Sitting on the small love seat across from her, Elizabeth wiggled to the edge. The aged leather screamed loudly against her friction. She fastened her eyes to Kerrigan. "Thank you for your honesty. It's obvious to me that he loves you. May I ask why you've never been involved with anyone before Axel?"

Kerrigan exhaled a breath. "Axel is the first man I've ever cared for this deeply." Peering through the large window, she caught a glimpse of the men at a distance on the dock, her focus drawn to one in particular who wore a white cap. A swarm of butterflies attacked her stomach at the sight of him. Slowly, she fixed her gaze back on Elizabeth. "I've never been any good at dating."

"Why's that?" Elizabeth asked.

"I attract the wrong kind of men—the ones who are only after one thing." Kerrigan lifted the glass of iced water from a coaster on the side table, brought the rim of the glass to her parched lips and gulped hard.

"Hmm, interesting. How many wrong men have you … hmm, encountered?"

Kerrigan slapped her hand over her mouth to keep from spewing the water she had swigged everywhere. She swallowed hard. "Oh! No. When I met Axel, I was a virg ... " She didn't think her heart could pound any harder or that she could be any closer to spontaneous combustion.

Curious eyes met Kerrigan's. "You were a virgin when you met Axel?" Elizabeth asked.

Her face lowered and covered with one hand to avoid Elizabeth's penetrating stare, the seconds passed slowly, the hands of the miniature grandfather clock on the mantel ticked along in amplified torture. "Yes." Kerrigan uttered softly.

The room became completely silent. Even the grandfather clock seemed to hush.

"I must admit, I'm comforted knowing that you haven't had … let's just call them 'prior experiences' before dating my son." Elizabeth cleared her throat and raised an eyebrow. "I presume you're more experienced now."

Kerrigan brought her knees to her chest, balling herself up on the sofa as small as possible. "Yes." She barely found her voice. She nervously twirled her hair and kept her head down.

"I'm sorry, dear. I don't mean to get so personal, but Axel is my son. I've always been sensitive about Axel and women. I don't want him to get hurt. He's had some … difficulties in the past."

Her head rested against the soft, cool leather. "If you mean Sara, he told me all about the whole awful thing." She gladly switched subjects.

"Yes, Sara," Elizabeth snarled and balled her slender fingers into a fist.

"You'll understand the protection a mother feels one day when you have children of your own. Do you want children?"

"Someday, but in the proper order," Kerrigan said. "Dating. Love. Marriage."

"You seem to have a good head on your shoulders. Do you plan to marry my son?"

The question hit her in the gut like a battering ram. Having his mother ask the very direct question was horrifying. Kerrigan hadn't even allowed herself to entertain the thought. She sipped her water again. The bristling leaves her distraction, her eyes stayed fixed outside. "We're taking things one day at a time. I care for Axel, and he cares for me. He hasn't made any serious indication of his intentions in that regard, and I'm not pressuring him."

Elizabeth smiled warmly. "I'm not trying to be terrible. You're a sweet girl. I can see why he loves you. I just know my son. When that boy of mine gets something in his head, resisting is useless." She shook her head.

"Yes, I'm learning that." Eyebrows raised, Kerrigan smiled, this time glancing at Elizabeth.

The women chatted the rest of the day. Elizabeth told her stories about Axel—embarrassing things that would have made him cringe had he known.

Standing in front of the wood beam mantel, Elizabeth's fingers traced the edge of a silver picture frame. She stared at the photo of an adolescent Axel standing next to his father, both holding fishing poles and broad grins plastered across tanned faces. "When Axel was a teenager, I asked him why he never brought home any of his dates or introduced us to any girlfriends." She whipped around to Kerrigan. "Do you know what he said?" The long cream dress Elizabeth wore and her long hair flowing down her back made her appear angelic.

"What did he say?"

"He said he wouldn't waste time introducing the family to a girl who was only temporary in his life."

"That's pretty insightful for a teenager."

"Yes. He's always been very serious about relationships. I asked him the same question on his thirtieth birthday. He said he'd only introduce the family to the woman he felt was wife-worthy—his words, not mine." She paused, her eyes glinting. "Well, here you are."

Speechless, Kerrigan's insides twitched. This was too much to process now.

"If Axel didn't see your relationship moving forward, you wouldn't be here. I'm sure you know exactly where you stand with him." Elizabeth shook her head. "He's always been brutally honest with women—good or bad."

Afraid of her own feelings, Kerrigan wouldn't tell Elizabeth that Axel had already said he wanted more with her and had even hinted at marriage. Maybe there was reason to hope.

***

Later in the afternoon, the men returned from fishing. Ryker proudly displayed his prize largemouth bass. To prepare the evening meal, Elizabeth brought in Chef Miguel Santos. Axel was right. His mother never worked a day in her life, not even to prepare a meal for the family.

The porch's outdoor fireplace crackled, drowning out the hum of insects, rustle of nocturnal animals climbing and clawing, and the creak of branches under the foot of creatures scurrying.

John placed his fork down and pushed back from the dinner table. "Well dear, that was a great meal." Rubbing his full belly, the edges of his mouth turned up, and his eyes landed on Kerrigan. "Did you enjoy yours?"

"Yes, sir." She glanced at Ryker and then at Elizabeth. "That was the best baked fish I've had in a long time."

Axel quietly observed, his handsome face graced by a serene expression. His longing eyes stared at her the same way they had in the account managers meetings week after week until he stopped attending. The petals between her thighs dampened on command of his gaze.

Even the roar of the outdoor fireplace wasn't enough to charge the crisp night air, the temperature dropping by the minute. A chill crawled up her spine, and she shivered. She glided her hand up and down her arms, creating warmth from the friction. Axel scooted his teak wood chair closer to hers and placed his arm around her shoulders.

"That's the oldest move in the book. Why not offer her your jacket?" Ryker threw his head back and let out a hearty laugh.

"I don't have a jacket. Besides, if I wanted to make a move on Kerrigan, this is what I would have done." Axel lifted her chin and covered her lips with his. She was glad she sat. Otherwise, she would have fallen to the floor as her knees buckled. Pulling away reluctantly, "That's how I'd make a move." Axel flashed a wicked smile, every inch of her flesh tingled.

Elizabeth stood. "Time to clean up. Anyone care to help?" She winked at Kerrigan.

"Come on dear, I'll help." John piped up. "Ryker, you too."

With everyone gone, Axel leaned in closer and kissed her again. Slowly peeling his lips away, he grinned as wide and as long as the planks of wood on the deck. "Enjoying yourself?" Flustered, she opened her eyes. "Yes. I'm having a great time. Your family is wonderful." For the first time since their arrival, Kerrigan relaxed.

His large hand caressed her cheek, and he smiled. "Everyone loves you. Me especially."

***

They walked the streets of the small town, and Axel held Kerrigan's hand in his. He led them into quaint boutiques, looking for nothing in particular. The first stop was an antique shop, and the next stop was an art gallery, places he thought Kerrigan would appreciate. Next, he led them to a jewelry store.

The glass-enclosed cases sparkled with brilliance, the light of the elaborate crystal chandeliers shined and bounced off exquisite stones and metals, that came in every variety, from sapphire to diamond and gold to platinum. Feigning innocence, he walked to the case filled with engagement and bridal rings, loitering there until she strolled over to join him.

"May I help you sir?" A tall and spindly man asked from the other side of the counter.

"We're admiring your jewelry." He glanced at her from the corner of his eye, slyly watching her as her eyes darted across the rings until they lingered. He made a mental note of the rings her eyes paused on, noticing they were the smallest ones in the case. When the time was right, he would do better than that. She deserved the best.

"Sweetheart, I see you like the princess cut style. Aren't they beautiful?" he asked.

"Yes, they are," she blushed when she realized that he had seen her looking at the engagement rings.

With his mission accomplished, he continued his conversation with the salesperson, the chatter of other customers in the background.

"I'm looking for a promise ring for my girlfriend." He smiled down at Kerrigan. She met his gaze, her eyes bulged, and breath was labored.

"Sir, those are in the next case over. What size ring do you wear, Miss?" The gangly man addressed Kerrigan.

"Oh. I don't know. I'll have to be fitted. I don't wear a lot of jewelry," she replied, giving Axel a quizzical look. "You don't have to buy anything for me." She whispered.

He grabbed her around the waist, pulling her into his side. "Sweetheart, I want to purchase a ring for you to express my feelings. See anything you like?"

She blinked a few times but didn't respond right away. He studied her face intently and then leaned down, and kissed her gently on the forehead, whispering in her ear, "Baby, I want the world to know that you're promised to me. Will you wear my ring?"

Nervous eyes peered back. "Are you sure?" she asked.

"I'm absolutely sure." He smiled brightly.

"Oh … Okay." She looked at the rings and selected a diamond studded, heart-shaped ring in white gold.

The clerk held out his hand to her. "Miss, may I see your right hand? We'll size your right hand ring finger." She held out her hand, and the clerk slipped the ring-sizer onto her long slender finger.

"You wear a size 6. I know I have this ring in your size." His kind smile reached the corners of his eyes.

"Great. That's the one we'll take." Axel pulled out his wallet and handed the man his credit card. He was glad she would wear his promise ring, but his real intent was to find out her ring size.

"Very good. That will be sixty five hundred dollars plus tax."

Kerrigan gasped, and her hand flew up to her mouth. "Axel, you can't spend that kind of money on me," she pleaded.

Hovering over her, he whispered to her. "Sweetheart, I can afford the ring."

She smiled and looked up at him. "I know, but that's …" Before she could finish her response, the man returned with the receipt and the ring. Axel took the box from the man, lifted the top and removed the ring. Taking her trembling right hand in his, he held her gaze and slipped the ring onto her finger.

"Kerrigan, this ring is a symbol of my love for you, and a promise of many good things to come in the future." He lowered his head, closed his eyes and everything around him faded to black, except her. Her small hands on his chest clinging to him for strength winded him. He breathed in her sweet fragrance as he captured her soft lips with his tender kiss. She pulled away, dazed, staring helplessly into his eyes. "I want you to wear it every day, for me, baby. Promise me," he said.

He knew she wouldn't reject him now. He owned her heart even though she wouldn't admit that she loved him. "Thank you, Axel." Her voice was shaky. "I'll wear the ring for you every day. I promise." She beamed with trembling lips and tears pooled in her eyes.

Coming from out of nowhere, Ryker sneaked up behind Axel and whispered into his ear. "One ring down, two to go."

Axel flung himself around and narrowed his eyes at Ryker, silently reminding him that he would make good on his earlier promise if he stepped out of line.

She lifted her hand and showed off her ring to Ryker. "What do you think?" she asked.

"Absolutely beautiful, Kerrigan. My brother has good taste."

Ryker meant that in more than one way.

***

They left the jewelry store and made their way to an ice cream parlor, the sugary scent tempting their taste buds to try an assortment of flavors. Seated at a round aluminum table, Axel and Kerrigan fed each other, teasing playfully as though they were the only two people in the world. In all his life, he had never behaved this way, never felt this way. Being in love was great.

Ryker rolled his eyes. "If you don't stop this humiliating public display of affection, I think I'll vomit," he said, and then pretended to shove a finger down his throat.

"Jealousy is a horrible trait that looks ugly on you my friend," Axel replied.

At that moment, a loud group of women scampered into the shop. "Axel? Axel Christensen? That is you," a woman screeched, turning Axel's head in her direction.

He instantly recognized the sound that came from the tall blonde woman. His lips pressed together, jaw clenched and eyes narrowed.

"Oh my goodness! Axel Christensen! It's such a small world. I haven't seen you in ages." The shrill of her nasally, high-pitched southern drawl, made his ears bleed. Looking back at her entourage as she slithered out of the time capsule, the 1990 Dolly Patron wannabe moved closer to where they sat, her hot pink heels clanking against the ceramic tile.

He didn't say a word. He glanced at a frowning Kerrigan, tightened his grip on her and squeezed her hand. Charlotte was a loud ball of energy, one of the many things about her that annoyed him. Charlotte's gaze poured over the couple and flinching, she stiffened. Catching Axel's eyes, she parted her lips, but nothing came out. He had to establish control.

"Hello, Charlotte. It's been a while. I hope you're well."

"I'm great, Axel. Looks as if you're doing okay yourself," she sneered at Kerrigan.

"Charlotte, this is my girlfriend, Kerrigan. Kerrigan, this is Charlotte. Uh, we're old friends," Axel replied tersely.

"Hi there, uh, Keri-gain, is it?" she said slaughtering her name like a butcher wielding an axe in a field of cattle. "Ax and I go way, way back. We dated off and on for a long, long time. We had some real good times, didn't we Ax." She winked. Snickers and giggles came from the three women who accompanied Charlotte.

He squeezed Kerrigan's hand again. He wasn't sure what she must have been thinking, but this wasn't good. Charlotte Monroe was the last woman he ever wanted to see again, especially with Kerrigan in his company.

"That was a long time ago Charlotte. It's been at least five years," he replied coolly. Charlotte was rude, loud and spoiled. Truthfully, he had only dated her for sex, a fact that he had been upfront about. He broke it off when she wanted to get serious.

Still holding Kerrigan's hand, he lifted their hands from under the table and placed them on display hoping Charlotte would see the promise ring. The woman irritated him like no other, from the shriek of her voice to her bodacious advances on him when they dated.

With an unctuous response, she leaned down pretending to want a better look at Kerrigan's ring. "Look at that darling little ring. That's the cutest little thing I've ever seen. I didn't know they made diamonds so small."

Ryker scowled at Charlotte, glaring with fiery eyes. "Charlotte, my brother didn't give you a ring, did he? I guess there wasn't anything to promise. Weren't you sleeping with half the town? Aren't you still sleeping with half the town?" He eyed her and then shot a look to the women standing behind her who covered their mouths with their hands.

"Ryker Christensen, you are the most ill-mannered man I've ever met." Charlotte's face flushed a shade of red nearly as deep as her garish lipstick. "Keri-gain, it was good meeting you.

Axel, keep your brother on a leash." She whipped around, her knock-off designer handbag flapping behind her as she scooted off.

He nodded his head. "Thanks, bro," Axel chuckled.

Axel turned to Kerrigan. "Baby, I'm sorry about that. We can exchange your ring for something bigger—whatever you want. The thing with Charlotte was a long time ago." He searched her face, hoping she wasn't angry or upset.

She looked up at him with her round hazel eyes, the edges of her mouth twisting in an upward curl. "Axel, I love my darling little ring with all its tiny little diamonds." She placed her hand on his chest. "This is the one I want. I don't need anything more than this."

His chest tightened at the dual meaning of her words.

***

Sunday, October 7

The cabin weekend ended late Sunday afternoon. They all said their goodbyes and went their separate ways. The ride back with Axel had been comfortable. She wasn't sure how their relationship and interactions would progress once they returned to life as normal. They arrived in the city before nine o'clock in the evening. He had invited her to stay the night with him at his house, but she was hesitant. She didn't want anyone from the office to see her and Axel ride in to work together. He pulled the SUV into her apartment complex and they sat in the parking lot.

"Kerrigan, I don't like that you are living alone in this apartment. Besides, I think I'm getting used to you in my bed at night. I may have to kidnap you again. Things worked in my favor the first time," he said, smirking.

She rolled her eyes and laughed. "Yes, things did work in your favor. What more could you possibly want?" she asked.

He pursed his lips and nodded his head. "So much more, baby. You have no idea." The look he gave her sent a shiver up her spine. She wasn't about to go down this path with him, so she didn't say another word on the subject.

They walked hand in hand to her front door, but when they stopped, Axel refused to release her hand. Finally breaking free of his grasp, she opened the door and walked into her apartment. She spun around in the doorway to face Axel, who was only inches away. He leaned down and brushed her lips lightly with a soft kiss.

"I'm not inviting you in. I know what will happen if I do. Neither of us will get any sleep, and we both have lots of work to catch up on tomorrow." She patted his chest gently, hoping to soothe him.

"Well, expect to be called up to my office tomorrow for a special closed-door meeting," he returned, giving her a sinister grin. Kerrigan felt a swarm of butterflies in her belly, and her cheeks warmed.

"You wouldn't! Brenda sits right outside of your office."

"I will. My office is soundproof, and I have an en suite bathroom, equipped with a luxurious shower for such occasions. Do you know how long I've wanted to have you in my office? I suggest you bring extra panties. I can't promise you'll leave with yours intact."

He pulled her close, gripped her behind and kissed her deeply. She could feel herself getting lost in his kiss, and she tore herself away. "Goodbye, Axel. I have a lot to catch up on. I'll see you tomorrow." She pushed him away playfully.

"Goodnight, baby. Lock your door. You never know who might come knocking in the middle of the night. Don't forget to bring the panties tomorrow."

"I'm not answering my door tonight, especially to sex-hungry lunatic boyfriends. I've had quite an active weekend, and I need to recover." She giggled as she watched him walk back to his car, glancing over his shoulder at her every few steps as he mouthed the words 'I love you'.

Later that night when she climbed into bed, she checked her emails. He had already sent her two meeting invitations, each scheduled for an hour and a half long at eleven o'clock and then at five o'clock. They were simply labeled 'Time Together.' She laughed, turned off the lamp on her nightstand and fell fast asleep.

CHAPTER SEVEN

Monday, October 8

Stepping off the elevator on the eighth floor, Kerrigan caught Megan's icy glare as they walked pass each other in the elevator lobby. Amanda from accounting leaned against the counter in the break room. Staring, Amanda walked out with a huff when Kerrigan entered to make her ritualistic morning coffee. On the way to her office, she caught the wide-eyed gaze of Matthew, one of the account reps, who turned in his seat doing a near 360-degree head spin as she passed by his cubicle. Although difficult, she managed to ignore them all.

She sat down at her desk, checked her email and learned that a meeting with McBride had been finally scheduled for the following week. Ages had passed since she had thought about the account. She needed to get back into the normal flow of her routine again and pull off a victory with the McBride account, which would not only validate her in the role that she had been promoted to, but would also get certain co-workers to back off.

At ten o'clock, Ashley peered through the door, and Kerrigan motioned her in. She closed the door and tossed herself into the guest chair.

"Hey girl! Word on the street is that you and Axel went away together last week, and not just for business. So?"

She rolled her eyes and huffed. "Ash! How do these people have time to be wrapped up in my personal life! How do they know?"

"Well, Marie found out that you and Axel would be out of the office last week. Brenda wouldn't tell anyone where the two of you had gone. The rumor mill was crazy. I heard, at one point, you and Axel ran off together, and he was selling the business."

"That's ridiculously absurd!" She sneered.

The last couple of weeks had been a whirlwind, and she had avoided thinking about what returning to work would be like. She hadn't thought to make up a cover story, but perhaps she could improvise.

"We were conducting research for the McBride account. We held focus groups on fishing products. How does that sound?"

Ashley pondered it a minute, scratching her temple. "For five days? I don't know."

"McBride is national. We were traveling to obtain regionally based sample data."

"Okay, maybe," Ashley said. Her voice was riddled with hesitation. "I might be able to work with that. Give me a day. I'll have those piranhas off your back in no time. Okay, so what actually happened? Where did you go? I want to hear everything. Every. Juicy. Detail." Ashley flexed her eyebrows up and down.

She shook her head at her friend and laughed. Even though the build-up to this point in their relationship had taken over a year, their relationship was hard to believe. Things between them were on warp speed now.

"So, are you still a virgin or not? I know he couldn't keep his hands off you. I want details."

She could feel her cheeks begin to heat. Just thinking about Axel made her warm inside. "Not." She paused, waiting for Ashley's loud squeal to subside. "My first time with him was … pretty intense. He was very patient and gentle. I'll just say that the experience was enjoyable." The corners of her mouth ached. A wide grin stretched across her face, uncontrollable, especially with Ashley's wild eyes staring her down. "Okay, this is embarrassing. I'm done talking about my days-old sex. We did other things, too."

Ashley leaned in closer, her elbows perched on the desk with her chin cradled by her palms. "Skip the other things. You gave your virginity to Axel freaking Christensen, and all you can say is that the experience was enjoyable? I. Want. Details."

She knew she was in full blush now. "Okay. Okay. He was unbelievably amazing. The rumors about his size are true, scared the hell out of me. Okay, that's about all there is to share. I'm not comfortable talking about this with you, so that's all you'll get out of me."

She told Ashley about the rest of the week she had spent with Axel and their trip to the cabin.

Ashley let out a shrill. "Kerri, that's beautiful. I take every rotten thing I've said about Axel back—well, almost everything. I'm so happy for the two of you. You know where this is heading, don't you?"

"Ash, one day at a time, please. I'm wearing his promise ring. That's enough for me right now." She held out her right hand and showed off the ring.

Ashley cupped her mouth. "He wants to be exclusive with you and he's already given you a promise ring. Seriously, what are you going to say when he proposes?"

"I'm still having a hard time believing that he wants a long-term relationship with me. I'm not even about to go there."

Just thinking about marriage gave her butterflies. She wanted to get married someday, but she had only thought about being with an average person, and Axel was no ordinary man.

"Have I been wrong so far?" Ashley asked.

She buried her face in her hands and mumbled into her hands. "No, but that's an enormous step. That's a forever step."

Thinking about forever with Axel would be foolish.

"Well, sounds as if forever might be his next step. This isn't the first time he's expressed wanting a future with you. The man introduced you to his parents, the first time he's ever done that with any woman. Hello! I'm just saying." She held up her hands in defense.

"Ash, I still have the most to lose if we don't work out. I am guarding my heart cautiously. You wouldn't understand."

Ashley shook her head. "I know he's been patient to this point, but even the most patient man tires out."

"Yeah, I know. So, how are you and Sam?" She needed to change the subject.

"Sam is nice, but he's not the one. He's just my flavor of the month. I might try CEO the next time!"

She rolled her eyes at Ashley before glancing at the clock. Butterflies danced in Kerrigan's stomach. Almost time to go to Axel's office for their eleven o'clock meeting. She heeded his warning. She brought a change of panties, but she needed to slip them into her bra, and she couldn't do that with Ashley sitting in her office. Some things she didn't share with Ashley. Axel scheduling time on their calendars for intimacy was one of those things she wasn't going to tell. At ten until the hour, she dismissed Ashley.

"Well, I'm glad we had the chance to catch up. I have an eleven o'clock, and I need five minutes to prepare for the meeting. Can we chat later? What about lunch tomorrow?"

"We'll chat later. I'm glad you're back. I'll take care of those rats out there. Lunch tomorrow, definitely."

***

Kerrigan walked into the executive suite, one hesitant step after the next on shaky legs. Brenda greeted her warmly. "Kerrigan, I'm so glad to see you. I hope you enjoyed your trip last week. Mr. Christensen said you had a productive week. You can go on in.

He's expecting you." Brenda's highly uncharacteristic chatty mood surprised Kerrigan, paused her steps.

She studied Brenda's face for a moment. "Thank you, Brenda," she said warily, still wondering what Axel had said about their time out of the office.

"Don't worry. I won't allow any interruptions, under any circumstances." Brenda smiled, nodded her head and returned to her computer.

Kerrigan didn't know why her nerves were threatening her sanity. She had been in his office many times before. This time was different, though, knowing what was about to go down.

She walked into his office and closed the door. Looking around the dark office, she noted that every blind on each set of windows had been drawn. Axel stood to her right, beside a bookshelf next to the door. Kerrigan pressed freshly manicured nails into the doorframe, keeping herself from slinking to the floor, his imposing stare her undoing. He swaggered over easy and casual until he was directly in front of her. Pinning her against the door, he reached around and twisted the locked. He didn't speak with audible words, but his wanton gaze spoke volumes. His eyes cascaded down her body greedily. She knew he loved to see her in a hip-hugging skirt and stilettos, and she dressed the part today intentionally. On command, her nipples perked up, and she was dripping wet with desire for him.

He took her into his arms and stared down into her eyes with his intense blue glare. He dipped his head, low to kiss her. He devoured her lips, acting as if he hadn't seen her in weeks. Whimpering and trembling at his touch, her knees buckled, under his spell. Taking her by the hand, he led her over to his red leather sofa on the other side of the room near his desk. Slowly, sensually, he unbuttoned her blouse, and then his fidgety fingers slinked to the back of her skirt. He smiled when he saw the extra pair of panties tucked neatly into her bra. "Good girl."

Unzipping her skirt, the fabric fell to the floor, and she stepped out. Axel leaned down to retrieve the clothing with one hand while his other hand tickled the inside of her leg until he reached the end of her thigh, caressing and stroking her sex through her wet lacy panties.

Tossing her head back, she whispered softly, "Axel."

He groaned into her ear. "Hmm. I want you in every way."

He tossed her shirt and skirt on his desk. His gaze combed her body. Perky caramel nipples peeked through a barely there teal lace bra. Like a shark preparing for a delicious delight, Axel circled around her in a seductive dance. His greedy eyes traced her long cocoa legs from the four-inch black patent leather stilettos up to a thin slither of lacy fabric that spanned her waist and descended at the base of her back, disappearing between two luscious, tightly toned cheeks. His tongue swiped across his lips. He couldn't wait to dive into her. He motioned for her to sit on the sofa and she complied. Axel's fingers slowly undid the top button on his white dress shirt, and then the next and the next until his shirt fell open, exposing every hard ridge of his tanned chiseled chest and the six-pack on his abdomen. He ripped the shirt away and threw it over his shoulder. Taking a step forward and then another until he stood directly in front of her with his strong, masculine stance, he lifted her hand to his crotch.

"Strip me." He commanded, bare-chested, and cock swelled in his black Oxford slacks.

Dropping to her knees, shaky fingers reached up, unfastened the button of Axel's slacks and then eased to the zipper. He covered her trembling hands with his, pressing her palm against his hard cock. She gasped. Her eyes nervously glided up to his. She gulped hard at the feel of the enormous bulge beneath her hands.

Axel met her timid eyes with fire behind his own. "This is all for you, baby."

Guiding the slacks down his firm thighs until they fell to the floor, he stepped out and then kicked the pants across the room.

"Sit back down on the sofa, baby."

A swift yank and he removed his boxers, stood hard and naked, giving her his nine-inch salute.

Axel kneeled on the sofa and lowered Kerrigan onto her back. Grabbing her ankles, he spread her legs wide open. Her right stiletto crashed to the floor with a thump. In one quick motion, he shredded her panties. Leaning down, he covered her wet center with his mouth enjoying the delicious nectar of her delicate flower as he sucked, licked and delighted in her sweet honey. She arched her back, involuntarily raising her hips high. Lapping at her juices as she freely flowed for him.

His hands kneaded her breasts. She was on the brink, but he wouldn't let her explode, stopping suddenly. He lifted himself and spread her legs wide, then slammed hard and deep into her. She gasped loudly and then covered her mouth with her hand. He smiled at her modesty. He pounded into her harder and harder, then faster and faster until her whole body shuddered. A frenzied hand massaged her swollen clit while his other hand squeezed and pulled at her hard nipples. He loved watching his pale cock disappear between her slick caramel folds and into her treasure. Her breaths fast and feisty, she moaned and whimpered as he continued pounding into her heat.

He had built-up sexually energy from the night before when he had to sleep alone without her in his bed. He hammered into her so deep and hard, she cried out in both pain and ecstasy.

"Axel, Axel! Please, no more."

He pinned her hands above her head with his. "Want me to stop?" He panted.

She whimpered, and her eyes rolled back. "Oh, god! Don't stop. Don't stop."

"Tell me what you want, baby."

"I don't know how much more I can take." She moaned. "Ah. So good."

Her reprieve, he pulled out temporarily.

"Baby, bend over. Hands on the back of the sofa." His voice was commanding but gentle, and she did exactly as he told her.

He pounded her hard and deep from behind. She could feel each inch of his sinewy apparatus reach the end of her. He moved in and out of her slickness, deeper and deeper until she cried out loudly. He reached around and covered her mouth with his hand to muffle her screams as he continued pounding her hard. He didn't plan to stop any time soon, and her screams only seemed to egg him on. He continued pounding her hard and deep. She dripped and leaked all over his shaft, down her thighs and onto the leather sofa. His incessant friction and deep penetration was too much for her.

"Axel, please. I can't take any more," she cried out.

"Baby, I want you to feel every inch of me inside you. Feel my desire for you."

He slammed into her harder and harder until no sound could escape her lips. His assault on her had never been so intense. His thick, long cock slid in and out of her, over and over again with such force that her legs shook uncontrollably. With every inch of him buried deep inside her, sweat streamed down her face, and her body convulsed all over. The intense pleasure of the orgasm lingered, not dissipating. Finally, her walls clenched tightly around his steel shaft in pure ecstasy.

Her legs trembled, and limp, she collapsed over the back of the sofa. Soon after, he exploded his seed deep inside her. He slumped down, his back against the armrest, and pulled her down to sit between his thighs. Her head rested against his heaving chest. He pulled her close, and stroked her hair back while kissing the crook of her neck as she floated back down from the ten-foot ceiling. He glanced at the clock.

"I guess I underestimated how much time we needed. I'm just getting started with you." It was already one thirty in the afternoon.

"Axel, I can't take any more today. Please." She panted nearly passed out as she lay back against his hot drenched chest.

"Kerrigan, did I hurt you?"

"You were a bit rough. I'm just too sore now."

Axel's brawny arms tightened around her clammy body. "Baby, I'm sorry. Having you here in my office is a fantasy come true. I was carried away. Can I do anything? Get you anything?"

"I need to recover for a few minutes."

"Stay with me for as long as you need. Would a warm shower help?"

"I think so."

"You rest now, and we'll shower later. I'll take care of you." He whispered softly into her ear. "I'm sorry, Kerrigan. I never want to hurt you."

She tilted her face up to meet the concerned look on his face. "I'm fine. You were intense, but you didn't hurt me. Every time we're together, you open me up to new heights." In his cradling arms, she rested.

Twenty minutes later, he eased himself from around her and held out his hand to help her up. She winced in pain as she attempted to move. He must have realized her discomfort.

"Don't move. I'll carry you," he said.

Axel lifted her up from the sofa, carried her into the bathroom and then gently put her down on the cold marble floor. Twisting the knob, he turned on the water, and then took her by the hand and led her into the shower. Too weak to stand on her wobbly legs, Axel held her up against his strong body. He washed her gently, admiring her body. She trembled at his touch. Foaming every inch of her soft skin with aromatic luxury body wash, the water flowed over them both, washing the scent of sex away. For several minutes, he cradled her in his arms before turning off the water. Softly, he dried her, gentle fibers of the Turkish towel absorbing the dampness from her flesh.

Dressed and her hair restyled, the only telltale sign that she had been on a romp with Axel was her missing lipstick. She dreaded walking into the executive suite lobby after being in his office for three and a half hours.

Preparing for Kerrigan to leave, they stood near the large suite doors. Embracing her from behind, her back against his chest, he leaned down and his mouth grazed the nape of her neck. "Kerrigan, I don't think this was a good idea."

She stiffened. "You didn't enjoy the sex?"

"No! That's not what I meant at all. I hurt you today. I had so much pinned up energy. I couldn't control myself. We can't do this in the office. I need you in my bed at night."

Kerrigan's small hand caressed his forearm and tensed at his admission. "I can't be in your bed every night. We'll figure out something." She glanced at the oversized office doors. "Do you think Brenda heard us?" she asked, horrified.

"I don't think Brenda heard anything. These walls are supposed to be reinforced and sound-proof."

She relaxed her stiff shoulders. "I sure hope so."

Axel tightened his arms around her waist. "I need you every night, Kerrigan. We need to talk about this soon."

She wasn't sure where he was going. Her pulse quickened.

Squirming until his grip loosened, "Okay, we'll talk soon. I have to get back to my office now," she said.

She spun around in his arms, tiptoed and met his kiss as he leaned down.

Axel's finger swiped the tip of her nose. "I mean what I said, Kerrigan. Soon."

Her eyes darted, avoiding his impassioned gaze. "Yes. Soon."

CHAPTER EIGHT

She was glad that Brenda wasn't sitting there when she finally walked out of Axel's office, thoroughly fucked. She made her way back to her office, trying to maintain a low profile. She hurried in, closed the door and pulled out her lipstick. Their relationship was still unbelievable to her. Just a few short weeks ago, she was a virgin who would do anything to avoid his imposing intensity and now she was in his office doing things she'd never even imagined. Being with him was surreal. How long would they last?

She continued working until five o'clock. She noticed that he hadn't canceled their late afternoon "meeting." She was under no circumstances going back into his office today. At a quarter after five, there was a knock at the door.

"Come in," She announced. When she turned around and saw him standing in the doorway, a hard lump formed in her throat. He walked in, closed the door behind him, and then stalked over to her desk. Her heart hammered in her chest. Was he out of his mind?

***

"Axel, what are you doing? We can't do that in here. Besides, I'm still sore." Her voice pitched.

"As tempting as the thought is, that's not why I'm here." His eyes narrowed, and jaw tightened, Axel pressed his lips into a thin line. His expression made her stomach wrench with pain.

He placed his hand under her chin, raised her face to his and leaned down. Suddenly, the office door flew open, and Megan marched in unannounced, and then she screeched to a halt. Axel slowly lowered his hand and turned around.

Megan stared with her mouth agape. "I, I'm so sorry, Mr. Christensen, Kerrigan. I thought Kerrigan was alone," she stammered, blood draining from her face.

"What do you need?" he asked sternly.

"I can come back later," Megan replied.

"No. Obviously, whatever you needed was so urgent that you burst into Kerrigan's office unannounced, which is not only rude, but also unprofessional. Now, what do you want?"

Megan's eyes darted from Kerrigan to Axel. "I, I just came in to find out about the trip last week. I was going to ask Kerrigan if she needed any help, with um, reports." Megan's stammering voice faded to a whisper.

"Oh? I didn't realize you were assigned to this project or on this team."

"I'm not sir. I just thought …"

He interrupted her before she could finish her response. "Megan, I know exactly what you thought. Let me make one thing clear for you. This is my company. What happens between me and Kerrigan is of no concern to you. Stay out of our personal business. All you need to worry about is your job and projects assigned to your team." He stood to his full height and moved so close to Megan that he could see as the tears formed in her beady eyes. "If I hear about you starting or spreading any more rumors about Kerrigan or me, I'll fire you on the spot with no questions asked. For the record, Kerrigan and I are involved romantically. I dare you or anyone else to say another word about our relationship.

Are we clear?" She nodded her head. "Now get out of this office," his voice boomed loudly, reverberating across the sea of cubicles.

Megan turned, making her exit as quickly as she could move. Tripping over her own feet, she fumbled to a near fall, gripping the edge of Kerrigan's desk, and then the wall before fleeing into the hall and closing the door behind her.

He softened his tone, lowered his voice and addressed Kerrigan. "Baby, that's what I came down to tell you. Brenda told me about all the gossip last week. She was concerned about how the rumors might affect you, us. I'm sorry, but this is my company and you are my woman. I won't stand for this behavior any longer. I'm not going to hide our relationship. Anyone who has a problem with us can leave."

***

Kerrigan's breath hitched, and her belly fluttered. "Thank you," she said, staring wide-eyed at him. Axel was her knight in shining armor.

Axel stood behind her and massaged her shoulders. "I'll always be here to protect you. Come on, sweetheart. Let's go home."

Coming to her feet, she picked up her handbag, and he grabbed her hand and led her down the hall. Silence fell across the floor as they made their way out hand-in-hand. Glancing around, she caught Ashley's smiling eyes.

They reached the parking garage elevator; he leaned down and kissed her gently on the forehead. She lifted her eyes to his, feeling herself beam all over. The elevator arrived, and they stepped inside. As soon as the doors closed, he swept her up in his arms.

She peered into his eyes. "Megan has been a nuisance for months. Before we were involved, she used to pass insinuating remarks all the time about how I was your favorite and how lucky I was to spend time with you. This is a giant weight lifted off my shoulders."

"She was right about one thing—you are my favorite." His smoldering gaze sent goose bumps prickling across her arms.

He moved one hand around her waist and cupped her behind with the other hand, massaging and kneading her cheeks as he pulled her into him.

"Axel, stop that! You can't have me tonight. I was nearly unconscious after our rendezvous in your office and I'm still sore. Stop that!" She giggled, and flushed.

He knew what he had done to her.

He stopped groping her and instead moved both hands to her waist. "All right, baby. Come stay the night with me and I promise to let you rest. I swear."

The elevator stopped, and he released her. They stepped out and stood in the parking deck, finishing their conversation.

"Uh, I don't know," she said hesitantly.

"Come on. I miss being with you and I can't sleep unless you're lying in my arms. I'm begging," he pleaded.

"Who would have thought that I'd have Axel Christensen begging me for anything?" She patted his chest. "Okay. I'll take pity on you this time."

He pumped his fist in the air. "Yes!"

She shook her head, laughed and rolled her eyes. They walked to his Range Rover, and he opened the passenger door, and then helped her climb inside before walking to his side of the vehicle.

He closed his door and started the engine. "I'd beg for you any day. You're going to pay for that," he said with a devious grin. Then he opened the sunroof.

"Axel, you swore! Seriously, I can't tonight," she squealed.

"Miss Mulls, you have a dirty mind. I can punish you without sex being involved. You'll find out soon enough."

"I don't have a dirty mind! And why am I being punished?"

"Because of the position you've put me in. I've never begged for anything from anyone, ever."

"I guess you're in unfamiliar territory." She lightly touched his arm.

"Very," he replied before grabbing her hand.

He stared deeply into her eyes. "Kerrigan, I mean everything I've said. I've never felt about anyone the way I feel about you. This is new territory for me, and I'm not afraid. I don't want this feeling to end."

She gulped hard, not sure what to say next and uncertain where he was going with his comment. The same old nagging thoughts of self-doubt returned. *Don't read too much into his words. Someone like him doesn't get serious about someone like you for the long haul. This is only temporary.*

She decided on the safest thing she could muster. "I'm in unfamiliar territory, too."

He leaned in and kissed her slowly, sucking her bottom lip. Her tongue tangled with his. They were lost in each other, falling deeper until he stopped and pulled back.

"I guess that means we have to figure this out together." He smiled and moved his hand to her thigh. "Are you sure there's no way I can persuade you tonight?"

"No!" She swatted his hand gently.

"You can't blame a guy for trying. Let's go home." He referred to them going home, made her wonder, if she were foolish to hope for a future with him. A future that held promised permanence.

***

That night, they ate the supper that Emma had prepared and left for them. After their meal, they settled down in the family room, cozying up on the charcoal microfiber sofa.

"Let's watch some television. I have no idea what's going on in the world these past few weeks." He flipped through the channels.

"Can we watch a mix of real news and a little entertainment?" she asked, batting her eyes at him.

"My thoughts exactly. A little Hollywood, a bit of Washington and a snippet of the local flavor."

"Perfect." She snuggled against him, resting her head on his chest.

"Of course, no evening is complete without a little reality television. Sad, but that's my vice." He confessed.

"I love reality television as long as the show has something to do with food, singing or humor. No blind dating or crazy personal drama."

He kissed the top of her head. "How about CNN, the Voice and Top Chef?"

"You've got a date. Since you're accustomed to staying up late, maybe later tonight we can tune into the local news and catch a little comedy," she said. "Do you like Tosh.0 or Chelsea Handler's show?"

"I knew there was a reason I love you so much." He squeezed her arm and laughed.

At nine o'clock, he turned off the television. "I'm going to work out, and you're going to join me—your punishment."

"That's my punishment? Bring it on," she retorted, confidence in her voice.

He flexed his pecks up and down. "Sweetheart, look at this body."

"I'm quite familiar with your body, thank you very much. Obviously, you have forgotten what my legs look like. I'm pretty sure I can keep up with you." Her toned muscular leg stretched across his lap.

He grabbed her leg firmly, and then pushed her back onto the sofa, arching over her and tickling her mercilessly.

She panted heavily between laughs. "Ah! Axel. Stop. Stop it." She laughed more.

Moving his hand away from her side, he sat up. "Woman, you are such a tease. Let's go, before I break my promise."

***

When they walked into his home gym, she remembered her first night at his house when she had accidentally spied on him from the guest bedroom's balcony. She never imagined that her relationship with Axel would blossom in this way. Glancing out of the window, she fixed her eyes on the balcony.

"You've upgraded your view. Would you like an up-close-and-personal show?" he asked.

Not waiting for her response, he peeled his shirt off and lied flat down on the bench press. His muscles rippled and strained as he pumped the heavy weights with all his strength. She gawked at him, her mouth agape.

He lowered the bar onto the rack, and the weights clang loudly. "Sweetheart, are you going to stand there staring at me all night?" A broad grin spread across his lips. "If you can keep up with me in here, you can keep up with me in the bedroom."

"You're a cruel man. I'm going over to the elliptical where it's safe," she said, and then stuck out her plump bottom lip.

"It's never safe when I'm near you. Stop pouting or I'll bite your fat bottom lip."

Butterflies danced in belly. She almost wished he would make good on his threat. Almost. She tucked in her lip.

"Fine. You want a workout?" She bent over, her firm round lobes perfectly positioned in front of him. "I'll need to do some stretching."

He sprung up and pursed his lips. "Careful where you put that beautiful ass of yours, Kerrigan. I'll wear you out worse than any workout in this gym if you keep tempting me."

"I thought you were a man of your word." She teased.

"I am, but the truth is I'm easily torn from my convictions in your presence. Tempting me is not a good idea."

Sweaty musk filled the air, their hot bodies pumping and straining to complete physical exertion.

An hour and a half later, they retreated to the house, heading for his bedroom.

***

Outside of his room, he paused. "You shower in my bathroom. I'll use the guest bath down the hall."

Back from the guest bath, Axel leaned against the doorframe, observing her quietly. Kerrigan was already in bed hammering out work on her laptop. The sight of her sitting in his bed, his heart swelled. He clambered into bed next to her. Even though they had slept in the same bed together many times before, tonight felt like a milestone. It was a work night, and there would be no sex. They were a normal couple. He liked the idea.

At eleven o'clock, she put her laptop away.

The lights turned off, he pulled Kerrigan close to him, enjoying her scent. "Hmm. Baby, I love holding you close, how your body presses into mine." Her small hand on his chest made his flesh sizzle. "This feels good, natural. Do you like this?" He never wanted the feeling to end.

"Yes." She agreed and nuzzled her face against him.

The word rolled off her tongue like a waterfall cascades over a cliff. When the time was right, he hoped she would say yes to his ultimate question with such ease.

***

Don't get too comfortable, her inner voice told her. The thought tormented her. She lay awake for an hour in the cocoon of his arms, unable to shake the feeling of impending doom and heartbreak.

CHAPTER NINE

Tuesday, October 9

When they arrived at work the next morning, Axel walked Kerrigan to her office. He made a point to make their arrival together known. Just inside her office, he leaned down and kissed her swiftly on the lips, careful not to lay the kiss on too heavy, for both their sakes. He wasn't concerned about professionalism. He knew they couldn't have a repeat lovemaking session as they had in his office the day before. A deep kiss would leave him wanting and unable to fulfill his needs or focus for the rest of the day.

"Sweetheart, we'll go home at five. I'll see you then." His statement was a command and not a question.

She didn't argue with him. She looked up at him sweetly. "I'll be ready."

***

He used the word *home* again.

Nothing out of the ordinary happened all day. She chuckled to herself thinking about Megan's facial expression when he confronted her the day before. The dynamics in the office were improved instantly.

Ashley was herself. At noon, the two women went to lunch to catch up. The topic of conversation would be her and Axel, of course.

"Kerri, I thought I was going to fall out of my chair yesterday when Axel busted Megan." Ashley laughed.

Kerrigan twisted her lips into a faint smile. "He was brilliant, wasn't he?"

"Obviously, he's serious about you, but his public outing of your relationship surprised even me. That's a very good sign. Remember what I said?"

"Yes, and that's a little scary. I'm comfortable with him, I feel as if I've known him my whole life. We … we fit."

"But?" Ashley tilted her head and raised her brow.

"Well, I can't help thinking it's just a matter of time before he's ready to move on. He says he loves me, but I can't say the words back. I'm trying to protect my heart."

"Kerri, too late for that. Just because you haven't said the words aloud, doesn't mean you'll be spared of heartbreak. Anyone with two eyes can see that he's in love with you, and you're in love with him, too. Face facts, Axel is done chasing woman, and you're the one he wants. That's a great thing."

"This is too soon. A few weeks ago, I still called the man Mr. Christensen. Isn't that crazy?"

"Hasn't he been after you for a while? I remember the way he looked at you your first day here. He began courting you from then, getting to know you better. Then he made his move. I would say he's been pretty darn patient."

"Okay, fair. Haven't you given me this same pep talk before? Let's talk about something else."

"I'll keep giving you this talk until you come to your senses. After all, if I don't look out for you, who will?" Ashley reached across the table and patted Kerrigan's hand.

"You know, he has a younger brother. He's cute. Maybe I should introduce the two of you. His name is Ryker."

Ashley shook her head in objection. "Oh. No. I'm not into younger men, and I've heard all about him. He's a total player."

Kerrigan laughed, and then changed the subject. "Okay. Well, how are things with Sam?"

"He still wants more than I can give him. I'm about to break up with him," Ashley said.

"I hope I get to give you a pep talk about some handsome hunk one day soon."

"I hope so too," Ashley said, and then laughed.

They finished their lunch and headed back to the office.

The rest of the day was routine. At five o'clock, he came to her office, and they left to go to his house. That night, they made slow and easy love all night long. She knew Ashley was right. Her heart already belonged to him. Though she hadn't said the words or allowed herself to accept the truth, she knew. She was madly and hopelessly in love with him.

***

Wednesday, October 10

Axel and Kerrigan were meeting Harris McBride at his office later that day. Kerrigan was nervous about this meeting. Taking long strides, she paced the length of Axel's office, clanking her heels against the hardwood with each step.

Thumbing through the presentation, Axel sat at the conference table. He watched her glide, the measured steps of her graceful gait. "Kerrigan, you're going to do an outstanding job. Stop worrying." He had practiced with her over, and over while he gave her pointers. She was well prepared.

She paused and pinned him with her eyes. "Thank you, but my nerves always get me going. I really want this account." Hands on her hips, she started moving again.

He didn't tell her that McBride probably wouldn't go for the proposal, especially since his soon-to-be brother-in-law was bidding for the same business. She had worked so hard on the presentation that he didn't have the courage to tell her the truth. He had to exchange a few favors just to get the meeting.

Pushing away from the table, he stood and caught up to her, hooking one of his arms through hers and spinning her to a halt to face him. "Sweetheart, I am proud of your work no matter what happens when we meet McBride today." Their bodies flush, he stared down into her eyes. "Kerrigan, this is damn good work and your presentation is the best proposal I've ever seen come out of this office. I want you to know that."

She gazed back at him with fire behind those big hazel eyes. "Thank you, but I want this. I really want this, Axel."

He pressed his lips together, clenching his jaw. He understood wanting something so badly, something that was within reach yet hard to grasp. He knew that feeling well. "Baby, you're ready. Let's do this."

She wore a killer St. John suit; the textured piqué pencil shirt clung to her curves while the caviar jacket accentuated her caramel hue. Four-inch, black and white Alice + Olivia Dina pointed-toe pumps ornamented her feet. He was glad he'd be joining her in case McBride got any ideas once he set his sights on her. As sexy as she was, he knew any red-blooded, heterosexual man would be crazy not to make a play for her.

Kerrigan had dug up as much research as possible on McBride, but the man was a mystery, even to Axel. She had found the general facts about McBride. He was a Princeton graduate and received his MBA from Duke. Single and in his late thirties, the man loved all things sports-related, especially fishing. With this knowledge, Kerrigan's genius in presentation form and her stunning beauty and charm, Axel knew they were as prepared as they could be. The rest was, well … up to McBride.

***

They arrived early at McBride's office for the two o'clock meeting. The executive lobby was reserved and formal, the sterile vibe quite opposite that of the eclectic, energetic atmosphere of A.C. Advertising.

"Good afternoon. May I help you?" The red-haired receptionist greeted them, peering up from behind a large L-shaped reception desk.

"Axel Christensen and Kerrigan Mulls. We have a two o'clock with Harris McBride."

"Oh! Mr. Christensen. It's good to see you," the woman said, staring at Axel. "Please take a seat." She batted her lashes.

"Thank you," Axel replied.

Kerrigan walked in first, followed by Axel. Harris McBride stood and extended his hand across a tidy cherry wood desk. Kerrigan's eyes followed the executive, a tall solid built man. McBride's gaze traced Kerrigan's form, his tongue swiping across thin lips. Axel closed the gap between them, took two steps closer to her. *Don't you see that ring on her finger?* He thought to himself. He knew the ring was on the wrong finger, but he was determined to remedy the situation as soon as possible. Harris walked from behind his desk, his hand stretched out to greet her first, and then he shook Axel's hand.

"Well, certainly it's a pleasure to meet you. *Miss* Mulls, right?"

Axel glared at him.

Her lips curl upward at McBride. "Yes. Thank you. It's a pleasure to meet you as well, Mr. McBride," she returned.

"I insist that you call me Harris. May I call you Kerrigan?" She nodded in agreement. Harris turned to greet him. "Axel, it's good to see you again. Please, take a seat." Harris motioned to them both.

Axel tugged at the collar around his neck, adjusting his tie. His blood began to boil, watching Harris ogle her.

He jumped in immediately. "Harris, we appreciate you opening your schedule to meet with us. Kerrigan has put a lot of thought into a national campaign that I believe will impress you. She's thoroughly researched the sporting goods retail market as well as the regional markets you've considered entering. I think you'll find that she's come up with a strategy that will differentiate your stores from your top competitors."

Harris turned to Kerrigan, his eyes roaming up and down her. "Great. I'm eager to see what you've prepared."

Kerrigan reached out her hand. "Here you are gentlemen, a copy of the presentation for each of you. I'll explain the details."

Taking her time to speak to each slide, she paused to ask if Harris had any questions and kept eye contact with him.

"You've just seen the data. Based on my research and thorough analysis of not only the regional market, but also on the demographics and behavioral trends of your target audience, I think Raleigh is an excellent market to enter."

Harris nodded his head. "Raleigh, huh?"

She leaned in close. "Of course, Mr. McBride, this is merely a recommendation and where you build your stores is up to you, but with Schooster going belly-up, sixty percent of the market is up for grabs." Harris' eyes glued to her. "You have the ability to swoop in easily and dominate that town, not to mention expanding your reach through online sales," she said.

Axel sat back with an elbow resting on the armrest of the upholstered chair and watched the pin-pong of words going back and forth between Kerrigan and Harris.

"And Mr. Harris, I don't have to tell what that means in terms of potential revenue." She shifted back in her seat.

Harris rubbed his chin and his forehead wrinkled. He turned to Axel. "She's good."

Her delicate fingers edged along the presentation until she flipped to the next page. "Now, let's talk more about the campaign and creative."

Axel was proud of her hard work and impressed with how she delivered the information with ease and confidence. After discussing the campaign's elements, she nodded her head, Axel's queue to discuss costs.

"I like what I hear. Miss Mulls, I must say I am very impressed and interested."

Axel knew Harris' interest wasn't limited to the presentation alone. He saw the way Harris watched her, how his eyes danced up and down her body, a look that he was familiar with considering he had the same initial reaction when he interviewed her. He wanted to reach across the desk and beat Harris to a bloody pulp, but he refrained himself.

"Kerrigan, your work is impressive. You've certainly given me a lot to consider. I especially like how you propose we handle the segmentation of our different audiences—very creative. I'm waiting for two other proposals and expect to make a decision within the next few months to coincide with our launch plans. May I keep this?"

Axel chimed in. "That copy is yours to keep. We're glad you liked it. Of course, we'll make any adjustments you'd like with consideration to budget and timeline."

"Great. Kerrigan, perhaps you and I can go over the finer details over dinner one evening." Harris' eyes raked over her body.

Axel leaned forward in his chair and glared at Harris, narrowing his eyes. He knew her beauty had a way of provoking men.

She glanced at Harris, and then Axel. "Axel and I would love to discuss details with you over dinner anytime you're ready."

"Harris, we won't take up more time than is necessary. I know you're busy." Axel rose to make their exit. "Thank you for your time today. I trust I will hear from you in the next few months on your decision." Axel extended his hand to Harris, and the two men shook hands.

"It's a great plan," Harris said as he looked at Kerrigan and reached out for her hand.

Harris regarded him with a curious look and raised his brow. "Axel, may I speak with you privately about another matter? I'll be brief."

"I'll wait outside," she announced, and then turned on her heel and strutted out of Harris' office.

Harris walked to the large window overlooking the East parking lot. "Axel, I have a question unrelated to business." He shoved his hands into his pockets and stared sixteen stories below. "What can you tell me about Kerrigan Mulls? She's smart, quite intriguing and beautiful."

Joining Harris' side, Axel cocked his head. "I can tell you that she's unavailable and very much taken," he replied coolly.

"That's a shame. She's one-of-a-kind. Do you know the lucky guy?"

"You're looking at him," he said more gruffly than he'd intended.

Harris looked embarrassed and shocked. "I had no idea. I didn't mean to offend you."

"I'm not offended. You didn't know."

"Well, I'll be in touch. Give my regards to Kerrigan. I hope you know how lucky you are."

"Thank you, Harris. And yes, I do know."

He met Kerrigan in the lobby, and they headed back to his vehicle. He opened the passenger side door and helped her in.

When he was inside, he turned to address her. "Congratulations, baby! You did a fantastic job. You did much better than I could have ever done. I think you have a real chance at winning the account."

"That's wonderful. What was that private meeting all about?" she asked.

"I had to clear up something for him."

"Is there a problem? Is everything okay?" she asked, her voice frayed.

"There was just a point of confusion on his part, something I plan to rectify soon enough. Let's go home and celebrate."

For the rest of the week, Kerrigan stayed at Axel's house. He didn't give her an option to say 'no'. He enjoyed her company and missed her terribly when she wasn't there. He knew what he wanted. It was time to set his plans into motion. He just had to wait for the right moment.

***

Saturday, October 13

When Saturday arrived, Kerrigan decided that she needed to go back to her apartment. She invited Axel along. "You know I'd love to go with you," he replied.

The Lexus rounded the corner and pulled into the guest spot reserved for apartment 1214.

He turned the ignition off, shifted in his seat, and his eyes darted down to hers. "We're going to have to stop going back and forth between my house and your apartment. You know how I feel about your living here alone."

"Then let's create a schedule. What if I stay in my apartment during the week and spend Friday evening to Monday morning at your house?"

He shook his head. "Kerrigan, I want more than weekends with you. What are we going to do about that?"

Avoiding his gaze, she toyed with the silver necklace that hung between her breasts, pulling at the heart-shaped pendant so hard that it almost snapped. "You can always spend a night or two with me during the week," she replied and moved her hand to the door handle.

Axel leaned across the console, his hot breath brushing her cheek and firm grip clamping down on her forearm. "That's not what I had in mind."

There was no escape. Nausea settled in her belly. "Axel, I don't know what you had in mind, but that's all I can do right now. Can we please go inside?" She whispered into his ear.

His lips pursed, he eased away and stared through the windshield. "I'll let you change the subject for now, but this isn't over. Let's go inside."

Startled by his harsh tone, her breath caught. "Okay. Let's go inside."

They walked into her dark apartment. She pulled open the white linen curtains in the living room, and then sauntered into the kitchen.

Trailing her step for step, he halted when she stopped. Axel leaned back against the kitchen counter opposite her as she riffled through empty cabinets. "Kerrigan, you don't have any food in here. My kitchen is fully stocked."

"There are these places called grocery stores. I can always go shopping." She scolded, her rear end pointed at him as she scoured the bottom shelf in the tiny pantry.

"Or, you can come home with me." He fired back. She came out just in time to see him flash his devious grin.

"Axel, this is my home. I'm an independent woman, and I can take care of myself."

He swaggered toward her, backing her against the counter, their bodies flush with one another. "I take pretty good care of you in bed, don't I?"

Kerrigan rolled her eyes. "Axel, you're missing the point." A warm sensation moved through her chest.

Long, masculine fingers ran up and down Kerrigan's right arm. "Am I? You know we're good together. Why don't you come and stay with me?"

She peered up at him, the palms of her hands pressed against his chest. "You'll never understand. I, I can't afford to lose myself in you."

He frowned. "I don't want you to lose yourself in me. I want you to give your heart to me."

"Axel, I have to keep my independence, and I ..." she paused, closed her eyes and shook her head, unable to find the right words.

He pressed his body firmly against hers. "Kerrigan, what you mean is you don't trust me." Axel pinned her in place, his hands resting on the countertop blocked her escape on either side.

She pushed her sleeves up, suddenly feeling quite warm. "I trust you to be the man you are. This is temporary. One day you'll snap out of your infatuation with me and then you'll be ready to move."

"What the hell is that supposed to mean?" He snapped. "I'm far beyond the point of us being temporary. And, I'm not infatuated with you. I'm in love with you, Kerrigan. At least I have the guts to say the words." His nostrils flared, and his body stiffened rigid against hers.

Nervous butterflies danced in Kerrigan's belly. "I'm an average person. You and I are from different worlds. You're Axel Christensen, and I'm just me." She pressed the palm of her hands against his chest, trying to put distance between them.

He grabbed her hands and held them close to his chest. "Kerrigan, there's nothing average about you. I'm a regular person. Why do you elevate me on a pedestal?" He sneered at her, waiting for a response.

She fixed her gaze on the upper cabinets behind him, averted his heated glare.

"Oh, I see. This has nothing to do with our differences or me. This is all about your insecurities. You refuse to trust me so that you don't have to let go of your fear or deal with your own feelings."

She lowered her head, blinking tears away. He was right again, but the truth was far more severe. The truth was that she didn't believe a man could love her truly—a belief she struggled with based on past failed attempts at relationships. She didn't know how to get pass the pain and hurt that she'd harbored for years.

"Axel, I thought we were taking things slowly? Why do you insist on pressuring me?"

Still holding her hands firmly against his chest, he lowered his head into the crook of her neck and muttered in a husky, raw voice. "Because, baby, I want more with you."

She closed her eyes and rolled her head back. "I'm not sure if I'm ready for more. I don't know what that means, and I'm afraid. I don't know what you want from me, Axel." She nearly moaned.

He straightened himself and leaned down so that his face was inches away from hers.

He softened his tone in reply. "I don't know what this means either, but I know I love you. This hasn't been easy for me either. I never expected I would fall in love."

He searched her eyes. "I want you to trust me. I want you to give me your heart. I want a future with you. I want it all with you, baby. I think you know what I want, what we both want." His lips covered hers tenderly.

Her heart hammered in her chest and her stomach flip-flopped as if she was in free-fall pushed from a skyscraper. She turned her head away. "Axel, I want the same, but I need time. Please be patient with me," she begged.

He brought his lips down to her shoulder, kissing her tenderly. "Sweetheart, you know I'll wait for you." He left a trail of kisses that seared her flesh, and then muttered into the crook of her neck. "I'll always wait for you, and until I can have you, I'll hold you close to me."

A single tear escaped the corner of her eye, trickling down her cheek and absorbed into his thick hair. Her fingers tousled his mane. "Please don't let me go. I … I…" She murmured under labored breathing.

"I'm not about to let you go. One day you'll say the words in your heart." He brought his head up and pierced her with his penetrating gaze. "Baby, why are you trembling?"

"You scare me." Tears washed her face. "I don't understand this. I don't get you."

He backed away and studied her in her complex, confused state. Then he grabbed her hand and led her down the hall to the bedroom. He climbed into bed and pulled her into his embrace, wrapping her in his strong arms.

After a long rest, he stirred. "Kerrigan." The sound of his deep voice rippled through her chest.

"Yes?" she questioned softly.

"There's no reason for you to be afraid." He pulled her closer. "There's nothing to understand." He stared into her wide eyes. "Baby, you can cry, throw a fit, have a meltdown, do whatever you need to do, but I'll be right here holding you through it all. I simply love you."

After the flood of tears stopped and she was done using his shirt like a box of tissues, he sat up. Glancing down at her he asked, "Do you feel better, sweetheart?"

"I think so," she said, nodding.

He lifted his shirt and tossed it to the floor. "Well, this needs a good washing."

She chuckled softly. "I'm Sorry."

Leaning down, he kissed her forehead. "That's okay, baby. I've see worse than snot and tears." He grinned. "I'm here to stay, and we'll get through this together. Let's get some sleep."

CHAPTER TEN

For the next couple of weeks, they followed the schedule. Kerrigan stayed at her apartment during the weekdays, and she went to Axel's house for the weekends. He missed being near her, so he made sure to spend two weeknights at her apartment. The arrangement worked well for her. Axel, however, was growing more and more impatient. He wanted more than sleepovers and wild romps in the bedroom. He wanted her for life. The thought scared him, but he knew where his heart was leading him. It was unnerving, and he was torn. The thought that she might reject him was terrifying. He did the only thing he knew to do. He called his father for advice. The phone rang incessantly until the deep voice on the other end answered.

"Hello son. It's good to hear from you. It's been awhile. How are you?"

"Good. How are you?"

"I'm fine. What's going on? You rarely call me directly."

"Things are good, very good, but I need your advice."

"Is everything okay with Kerrigan?"

"How did you know when you were ready to propose to mom?"

"I couldn't imagine my life without her. Other women ceased to exist in my world. It was only your mother. Is that how you feel about Kerrigan?"

"Yes, since the day I met her and my feelings have only gotten stronger. I want to spend my life with her."

"Well, you have your answer. When are you going to propose? Wait until I tell your mother. She'll be thrilled."

"Hold on dad. I've haven't made firm plans yet. Please don't say anything to mom. There's a strong possibility that I could be rejected."

"I've seen the two of you together. I know she loves you as much as you love her. Why would she reject you?"

"She's convinced that my feelings for her aren't real. She's insecure, scared."

"I'm no expert, but if you ask her to marry you, I don't see how she could doubt your intentions. Putting your heart on the line is the ultimate testament of your love."

He exhaled a breath. "I hope you're right, but I have to wait for the right moment."

"Son, you don't wait for the right moment, you create the right moment."

Like a beckoning light at the end of a dark tunnel, that simple statement was the clarity he needed to make his next move.

***

Saturday, October 27

The alarm clock buzzed loudly jarring Axel from his sleep. He hit the off button before the sound disturbed Kerrigan. He studied the delicate features of her face, a rare natural beauty that required no accessory, no make-up or jewelry. His fingertips ran gently along the dip of her waist to her hip, admiring her generous curves and toned body. He stroked his knuckles across her hairline, pausing at her sun-kissed cheek. She amazed him.

Panic seized him as his next thought formed. Winning her heart hadn't been the problem, getting her to give in to their love and to trust him was an entirely different matter altogether. He pulled out the little box from the top drawer of his nightstand and opened it, looking at the custom platinum, four-carat diamond ring inside. He closed the box and placed it in back inside of the drawer.

***

Kerrigan's eyes fluttered opened slowly, and Axel's grin came into view. He propped himself up on his elbow and hovered over her.

"Good morning beautiful," he greeted her.

"Good morning."

"Slept well?"

"What little I got, yes," she replied groggily and flashed a weak smile.

"I'll make no apologies for the little amount of sleep you got. You knew what you were in for last night," he replied.

"Not true. I had no idea what was going to happen," she said coyly.

He leaned down and kissed the tip of her nose.

"Liar. You knew I wouldn't be able to keep my hands to myself. Like this," he said as he grabbed her breast and kneaded it in his hand.

At the command of his touch, her nipple hardened. He lowered his head to kiss her, but she turned away.

She cupped her mouth. "No. I have morning breath."

"All right, let's go get you cleaned up dirty girl. Come on, we'll take a shower."

Axel handed a terrycloth robe to her, and then he put on his own. He couldn't keep his hands to himself, touching and tickling her as they entered the bathroom. As with everything else in his house, the bathroom was exquisitely designed. The room was larger than her living and dining rooms combined. Walls covered in a faint powder blue gave the modern bathroom a serene spa-like quality.

He paused by the sinks housed in rich, dark chocolate cabinetry. "Here's your toothbrush." Axel handed it to her and then grabbed his own. "Oh, and let me close the door," he said, remembering her quirk about closing the bathroom door whenever she brushed her teeth.

When they finished brushing their teeth, he sauntered passed paneled mirrors that ran the length of one wall to a series of switches on the wall. Although it was sunny out, he dimmed the room. One of the switches controlled the sensual melodic instrumental tune that pulsated in the background. The shower stood in the middle of the bathroom, encased by glass on all four sides. With the flip of another switch, the clear glass walls turned translucent. He removed his robe and tossed the cover onto a nearby wooden bench. His hands slid down her shoulders, unsheathed her and placed her robe next to his. Grabbing her tiny hand, he guided her into the over-sized shower. The ceiling-mounted rain shower cast a blue-green haze down into the shower.

"Have I told how much I love this bathroom? I especially, like the feel of the tumbled limestone floors under my feet. Your home is spectacular."

"Glad you like my style, especially since you'll be spending lots of time here. That's enough about the house. Let's get you wet." Axel pressed a button and the rain shower overhead drenched them, a steady stream of warm water washed their naked bodies.

He took her into a firm embrace, and their lips collided. Moist heat surged through her and flowed between her thighs. Lowering himself to the shower bench, he pulled her down to straddle him. He reached around and under her, stroking her slick wet entrance.

"You want this?" He gripped his mushroom-headed tip.

Aching to have him inside her, she moaned a whispered, "Yes."

He raised her up and gently lowered her down on his hard shaft. His pale length disappearing between her caramel folds penetrated and reached her end.

She gasped. "Ah! Axel." Clawing, her nails dug into his back.

"Kerrigan." He groaned.

Thrusting his hips in rhythmic harmony to the sensual music flooding the room, he pumped into her. Deep. Hard. Slow. She pushed down against him, rolling her hips and taking in the fullness of his thick rod. The intensity built inside her body until she writhed uncontrollably in his arms, her senses shattered. He rocked deep inside her, his fingers pressed into her fleshy lobes as he tightened his grip on her swirling hips until he exploded into her haven, joining her in rapture.

His cock still hard and buried inside her, Axel held her close against his chest in their heated afterglow. He didn't speak and she couldn't. Slumped over his shoulders, her shaky fingers clung tight as she fought hyperventilation. He nibbled on her ears, licking them as he tangled his fingers in her wet wavy hair. Eyes closed, she sucked in a quiet breath and stiffened, her heart nearly exploding at the intensity of his caress and attentiveness of his tender touch. A trail of kisses up her neck forced a soft incoherent mutter from her lips. Suddenly weepy, the cascading rain falling, the music filling the air, and the dimly lit room with the blue-green glow casted down from overhead overloaded her senses.

She fought tears back. She had fallen for him, hard, and there wasn't a thing she could do about it. She wanted him, wanted to give herself to him completely, yet she couldn't.

Breaking their intimate connection, he lifted her to her feet. They bathed each other, washing away the evidence of their passion. The rain from the showerhead beat down on her head, mingling with the tears. She hoped the droplets would camouflage her deluge. She didn't want him to notice that she had been crying. Frowning, his hands dropped to his side, and he searched her eyes. Then unexpectedly, he grabbed her into his arms. They stood naked locked in an embrace as he held her tightly.

He leaned down and looked into her eyes. "Baby, why are you crying?"

Head tilted and eyes cast down, "It's nothing," She avoided his stare.

"Don't lie to me. We should have honesty between us always. I want to be here for you, but I can't do that if you won't let me in. Now, tell me what's wrong." His voice strained.

"I don't want to spoil the mood. I'm fine. Please let this go, Axel."

Holding her at arm's length, he gawked at her. "No. We're not leaving this shower until you tell me. You're not a good liar, so you better tell me the truth."

She brought her hands up to her chest, the tears building rapidly. "I'm just overwhelmed. I'm trying not to be all caught up. When you're done with me, I don't ..."

He interrupted her, his head flinching back slightly. "When I'm done with you? Haven't you been listening to a word I've said? Haven't I made my intentions clear? Haven't my actions been clear?" She shook her head after each question, her expression blank. "Kerrigan, I want you." He frowned, his forehead stressed with creases. "You're the woman I've been waiting for and I want to spend my life with you. I know you need time. I want to give that to you. I don't understand why you have these insecurities, but I know we can work through them together." He scratched his temple and then dropped his hands to his sides. "I have long-term plans for us. I'm waiting for you to give me all of your heart. Why don't you believe me? Trust me."

She swallowed hard. She knew she should choose her next words carefully, but he had demanded the truth.

"You want the truth? Fine, then I'll give you the truth, but you're not going to like what I have to say. You're young, sexy and rich. You've always dated skinny blonds who look like super models. You grew up surrounded by wealth and rich people." Her voice choked with emotion. Flailing her arms, her darting gaze landed on the overhead shower fixture. "Look at the way you live, Axel. I grew up in an apartment, and I live in one today." Her pitch rose to a-glass-breaking-squeal. "I know we have many things in common, but we come from different worlds. I wonder if that will be enough." Axel's mouth dropped open.

She wrapped her arms around her stomach. "You went to an Ivy League school with no hesitation—no questions asked. I had to claw my way into one, and then fight like hell, to prove I deserved to be there. You sexualized me from the day we met. I wonder if that's because I'm a black woman. You say you're proud of my work. I wonder if that's because you had such low expectations that anything I did outside of spreading my legs would impress you." Axel eyes stretched wide, and he clenched his fists tightly at his sides.

The fire in her eyes blazed blue flames. "When we get stares and hateful looks, or when one of your friends says something negative about me or us, I wonder if you'll leave me and choose someone who's more suitable—familiar. I'm exotic to you now, but when my novelty wears off you'll be done with me and I'll be devastated. You don't love me. You love the idea of me."

Arms crossed over his chest, Axel blew out a hard breath, nostrils flaring. He dropped his head to his chest.

***

Axel closed his eyes, his chest heaving and the vein in his neck throbbing. Silent for a few moments, he absorbed the meaning of her callous words before responding. In that instant, he realized that she would make him out to be the villain no matter what he said or did or how he treated her. She wouldn't trust him, and he would never have her fully. Slowly opening his cloudy eyes, a single tear rolled down his red face to his clenched jaw. He wouldn't propose to her and be subjected to her cruel rejection. Steam rolled off the top of his head. Angry at her harsh words, he stepped away from her.

She reached out as he backed away. "Axel, please say something."

The muscles in his face strained to prevent collapse. "I have nothing else to say, Kerrigan. This is what you'll always think of me. You'll never give us a chance. You've made me out to be a shallow, self-centered man. No matter what I say or do to show you my love for you, you'll never trust me." His tone was low, barely above a whisper.

She reached out again, and his arm flinched back. "Clearly, you have a problem with our differences, or maybe you have a problem with my skin. I've never thought of you as average or as a conquest. I thought we shared something beyond the surface. What we've shared over the past year must have been meaningless to you. My love for you is hopeless and wasted."

He turned his back to her and lowered his head.

"Kerrigan, maybe you're right. Maybe we should just end this now. I never wanted to hurt you, but I can't live with your constant scrutiny and expectation that I will. I wanted more than a casual relationship with you. For the first time in my life, I wanted more." He closed his eyes. "You don't know how much you've hurt me."

She jumped at his hoarse laugh.

"Funny, you were so worried that I'd break your heart and instead you've broken mine. I loved you."

He stepped out of the shower, grabbed his robe and fled the bathroom leaving her in the shower alone. Even with the fresh wounds she inflicted, he didn't intend to let things end between them. He wanted to teach her a lesson. He knew she would be hurt. That was his plan. She needed to feel rejection, to feel pain, the same way she dished it out to him.

***

She slumped to the floor and tears poured from Kerrigan's soul. The finality of his words sunk in, his pain so potent that his reddened eyes pierced her heart. She shuddered all over, recalling his pained face and gritted teeth as he stared down into her eyes. She had never witnessed him be that angry. The love in his eyes had turned to fury. Did she allow her insecurities to destroy their relationship?

Kerrigan shivered, the streaming hot water had become cold. A trembling hand reached for the handle, turned off the water. She stepped out of the shower, dried herself and then pulled on the robe. Standing at the mirror, puffy eyes and a swollen face reflected back. She dragged her weak, quivering body into the bedroom. There was no sign of Axel.

A note lay on the crumpled sheets still sultry from their passionate lovemaking, where their bodies had been entwined. Her tears flowed again and she sunk to the floor next to the bed. This time she knew this wouldn't be a love letter. A wave of nausea washed over her as her shaky hands opened the folded piece of paper. There were only two sentences scribbled on the inside. Her heart dropped as she read the words.

Kerrigan,

I've gone for a jog and have some business to take care of. Thomas will take you home.

Axel

CHAPTER ELEVEN

The ride home was the longest ride of her life. The world outside whizzed by in a blurry haze. Kerrigan fought her tears the entire trip. She barely noticed when the car came to a stop outside of her apartment building. Thomas stepped out and around, and then opened the door. She didn't have much to carry since Axel had arranged for everything to be provided for her at his house.

Walking into her home was strange. Although only a couple of days had passed since she was there last, to her, a lifetime had passed. She meandered into her bedroom and changed into a pair of cream lounge pants and matching hoodie as was customary whenever she moped. The red light on her home phone flashed indicating she had messages waiting. She dialed into the system. After each message had ended, nervous fingers pressed the number one to hear the next message, hoping that one might be from Axel. None of messages had been from him. She knew from his reaction that she'd hurt him badly. She was hurting too. The worst part was that she didn't know what to do to fix the pain she had caused him.

The rest of the day, she sulked, ignoring two phone calls, one from Ashley and the other from her mother. She couldn't bear the thought of having to rehash the events that had unfolded between her and Axel. She knew Ashley would rip into her for screwing things up. Her mother didn't know anything about her relationship and conversation with her would feel empty and insincere.

At two thirty, there was a knock on the front door. Her heart leapt into her throat. The last time she'd received an unannounced visitor had been Axel. She jumped up. Jittery legs carried her to the door.

"Who's there?" she asked anxiously.

"Me, Ash. Open up Kerri. Are you okay?"

Her heart sank. She fought tears back and maintained her composure.

Ashley shoved passed her. "Where on earth were you? I've been worried sick. I haven't seen you in forever, and you haven't returned any of my messages. Is everything okay?" Hands on her hips, her eyes canvassed the room suspiciously.

"No, I'm not okay. It's over with Axel." Kerrigan wrapped her arms around herself.

Ashley gasped and cupped her mouth. "Kerri, what happened?"

She knew Ashley wouldn't make light of her situation. Standing in the small foyer, Ashley coiled her arms around Kerrigan, and then they strolled toward the sofa.

Tears pooled in Kerrigan's eyes, her limp limbs sank into the sofa, and she curled her knees to her chest. "I don't know how to give him what he wants. He wants a future with me. He wants me to trust him, to give my heart to him. I pushed him away. Now he's gone, and I don't think he's coming back."

Ashley plopped down beside her. "I thought he was willing to take things slowly and wait for you? What happened? Is he using this as an excuse to dump you?" Ashley's nostrils flared as she spoke.

"No. Nothing like that at all. He really cares for me. I know he's in love with me. I don't know how to get over the insecurities gnawing at my brain." She didn't know what it would take to trust him. Perhaps nothing would ease her insecurity. "How can someone like him want someone like me? He said he couldn't live under my constant scrutiny and expectation that he'd hurt me. This is my fault." She buried her face in her hands.

"Kerri, do you love him?"

"Yes, you know I do, but I've never said the words to him. I can't. I'm paralyzed by fear."

"Girl, you need to get over whatever is bothering you. A man like Axel comes along once in a lifetime, if at all. How is being with him? You both seem to have so much in common."

"Being with him is amazing. We laugh together, like the same things, want the same things. When we make love …" Her shaky voice pitched. "Making love is out of this world. He's romantic. Ash, I screwed up." She paused. The flood of tears overflowed down her cheeks. Barely audible, her voice strained. "I, I don't think … he'll ever take me back. I kept pushing him away. I said awful things to him. There's no coming back from that. I've hurt him too badly." She wailed loudly. Wringing her hands, she rocked back and forth in a fetal position until she sobered.

"If he really loves you, and I believe he does, then there's always hope."

She hung her head low, staring into her kneecaps. Her tears began to fall again. "I don't know how to go on. I don't know if I can work with him, see him every day."

"Can you ask to be assigned to a different project? Maybe things will blow over. This was just a fight."

"It was more than a fight. I've never seen him look the way he did. Ash, I think I should resign." She sobbed loudly. Maybe ending things between them was best. It didn't matter now. He had made the choice for them both. Perhaps this was the only choice that could be made.

"Slow down. Why don't you see how next week goes first?" Ashley patted her shoulder.

She lifted her head to Ashley's tender eyes and mouth drawn into a straight line. Kerrigan was silent a few moments before responding. "Okay. I can do that." It had only taken a few weeks to fall for the man. Perhaps she could get him out of her system in the same amount of time. She was a rational thinker. But love follows its own principles, and neither rationale nor logic was relevant in a situation such as this. And she knew it.

"Kerri, I've never seen you like this. Don't lose hope. Did he say you and he were over?"

"Not in those exact words, but close enough. He was extremely upset. He said that maybe we should end the relationship. He told me that I broke his heart."

"Give him some time. You just had a fight. Couples fight, and then they make up."

Ashley hugged her friend and then stood up. "I've got to get going, but I wanted to check in on you. Call me anytime. I'll see you Monday. Everything is going to be fine."

She dragged herself to the front door with Ashley. "Thanks Ash. I'm going out for some fresh air. Maybe I'll grab some coffee and think things over. See you Monday."

As soon as Ashley left, Kerrigan slipped on her pink and gray New Balance walking shoes and headed outside. The air was crisp and cool as she paced the nature trail. The crunch and crackle of mulch and twigs snapping under her feet reminded her of her broken relationship. Remembering their first meeting in his office when he interviewed her, their attraction had been instant. A slight smile paused on her lips as she reminisced, recalling their first unofficial date in the skybox. He had declared their friendship there. Recounting the many emails they had exchanged, he slowly revealed his feelings.

The first time she spent an evening at his house when he had essentially kidnapped her—the first time they made out on his balcony and then later in his office—these were all memories of two people falling in love. The memory of the picnic he had arranged for her made her heart swell. Throughout their entire relationship, his feelings had only grown and he had proven himself trustworthy. He loved her, he truly loved her, and she had been too wrapped up in self-doubt and pity to accept his love.

At a near sprint, a shrub grazed her arm as she made a beeline for her car. Her favorite place to decompress and think while sipping on a refreshing mocha latte beverage was a quaint coffee shop located near Axel's house. She would go there and clear her foggy head.

The coffee shop buzzed with people when she walked in. She stood at the counter eyeing the menu and glancing at the tempting pastries on display. "I'll take a medium-sized soy mocha latte." She was nursing her self-inflicted wounds. "Add a slice of banana nut bread, please."

The young man behind the counter rang up her order. "The bread just came out of the oven, so it's nice and warm." He smiled. "That'll be eight dollars and fifty four cents," he said, putting the bread onto a small plate and handing the latte to her.

She handed over her debit card. "Thanks." Kerrigan shoved the card into her jacket pocket and then grabbed her plate and beverage. Her eyes scanned the café, searching for a quiet, private spot. A short woman carrying a laptop bag was leaving a table in the corner, near the front of the shop. The spot was perfect—out of the limelight, and she could make an easy escape when she was ready. She sank into the large leather chair, placed her plate onto the chair's wide rectangular arm and sipped her coffee.

A group of obnoxious teens bolted through the doors laughing and making a loud raucous as they worked their way up to the register. Despite the distraction, a million thoughts raced through her mind as she people-watched and took bites of her warm delicious bread. Things were moving so quickly with Axel that Kerrigan had become scared. He meant everything to her. Interrupted from her thoughts again, she eavesdropped on a young couple that sat at a table near her. The man was apologizing for something he had done. Maybe she could go to Axel and apologize. She hadn't meant to hurt him.

From the way they stared at each other and how they touched, it was obvious that the young couple was in love. Was that how she and Axel looked to the rest of the world? She sipped her coffee. For the first time, she felt hopeful despite their fight, that their love could survive and that he was her Mr. Right. She was going to win his forgiveness and get her man back.

The deep thunder of a familiar voice snatched her attention away from the couple. Nervous butterflies fluttered in Kerrigan's stomach. Axel and a blonde walked into the coffee shop together, their backs facing her as they made their way to the counter. Who was the attractive woman with him? They stood in line chatting. They couldn't see her, but she saw them. Her heart hammered, and her hands turned clammy. She listened carefully to their conversation, making sure she wasn't overreacting. The woman's voice was distinctively sophisticated, obviously someone he knew from his circle. *Don't jump to conclusions. Listen to their conversation.* She told herself.

"I'm glad you're here. Thank you for coming. I'm sorry it's been so long. I've been preoccupied—Kerrigan," he said.

"I understand. You're ready to move on now. That's great." The woman responded as she reached for his hand. He didn't pull away.

"This is going to sound harsh, but I'm done with her. I got what I wanted. She's history to me. I wouldn't care if she dropped off the face of the earth. In fact, I wish that slut would disappear for good." His tongue spewed venom.

"Axel, does that mean I'll be seeing more of you?" Her voice hinted a smile.

He laughed and wrapped her in his arms. "You'll be seeing much more of me. I've missed you."

She had heard and seen enough. Kerrigan wanted to melt into her seat and die. Her stomach turned and knotted. She thought she might even vomit. A sheer force of will power kept her from bursting into tears. They walked closer to the counter, out of her earshot and out of sight. The first opportunity when their backs were still facing her, she leaped up and bolted for the exit. An elderly couple was almost victim to her stampede.

Outside, she ran down the sidewalk away from the shop's large windows to her car. Her hands trembled and chest heaved as she hyperventilated. She fumbled with the car keys and finally collapsed into the driver's seat. Covering the steering wheel, she buried her tear-streaked face in the fold of her arms, and then sobbed loudly, uncontrollable. His words were etched in her memory and echoed in her head. She knew she could never face him again. He had used her, hurt her, and she was devastated. She knew this day would come and here it was.

***

Still lying awake in bed at eleven o'clock on Sunday morning after a sleepless night, all Axel could do was to think about Kerrigan. In general, he didn't sleep well. She had become his solace. With the rift between them, his fits of restlessness returned, and they were magnified. He contemplated going to her apartment to talk, but decided against the act.

He crawled out of bed, showered and dressed, and then headed for the garage.

Rob was already seated when he arrived at the restaurant.

Axel slid into the booth across from his friend, his stubbly face twisted into a frown. "Hey." He groaned half-wittedly.

"God! What happened to you man?" Rob's forehead wrinkled. "Let me guess. Woman trouble."

"Hmm." Axel groaned. "That obvious?" He missed Kerrigan desperately. He missed her smell, the way she smiled, her laugh, her touch, her feel.

"I haven't seen you in weeks. Are you still pining after that hot little thing at the office?" Rob flipped through the menu, and then glanced up at Axel. "Kerrigan."

Just hearing her name made Axel's stomach twist. "Yes, Kerrigan. There have been quite a few developments since you and I last talked." He couldn't eat. Nothing on the menu was appealing. "We're dating. She's my girlfriend, or at least she was." Imagining his life without her was painful.

Rob's brows shot up. "Just dating? Judging from your appearance, I think you're more than just dating. Looks serious to me."

"I guess I'm an open book. Our relationship is pretty serious." He pushed the menu away and gazed around the busy restaurant. "I'm only getting coffee—not really hungry."

The waiter came and took their orders, and then they continued talking.

"Man, I've never seen you like this. What happened?"

"We love each other." She hadn't said the words, but he knew she was in love with him. "I want more, and she's insecure about herself and our relationship. She doesn't trust me. She threw out some bullshit excuse about me wanting to experiment." Axel rubbed his temple. "I was supposed to propose to her this weekend." Rob stared at his friend, listening, and then he took a sip of coffee. "She said some very hurtful things to me, and I stormed out on her." She had hurt him, and he had to teach her a lesson. If there would be a future between them, Axel didn't want Kerrigan doubting his love.

Shoveling a fork full of food into his mouth, Rob mumbled, "I'm sorry man. Do you think you can save your relationship?"

Axel's lips pressed into a tight line. "I hope so. I'm going out of town for a few days. The time apart might be good for us both." He wanted her to trust him, to have faith in him. He wanted to remain optimistic, thinking that somehow they could work out their issues.

Later that night, Axel crawled into his lonely bed, lost and confused. The realization that their relationship might not survive took a toll on him. His eyes heavy and tired, a lone tear dipped down his cheek onto his pillow, and then the outpouring—for the first time, he cried.

***

Monday, October 29

Monday hit like a brick thrown against hard pavement. Axel didn't want to get out of bed. He was exhausted, but he had too much work to do. When he had been on good terms with Kerrigan, he ran on pure adrenaline.

Peeling the duvet back, he dragged one heavy leg at a time over the edge of the bed. Forcing his muscles into motion, he stood and wandered into the bathroom, to get ready for the day.

Bittersweet memories of their last time together still lingered. He remembered holding her close. When they made love, their souls were joined. He had never experienced a connection so carnal, spiritual and emotional all at once. He had to have her back. He decided to make things right between them. They had both suffered long enough. He began to put plans into motion.

As soon as he sat down behind his desk, he called Brenda into his office.

Clunky steps hammered against the floor as Brenda made her way toward the large black desk. "Good morning. What can I do for you, sir?" she asked.

He met her patient eyes. "Morning Brenda." He growled. "Please ask Kerrigan to come to my office the minute she arrives."

"Okay. I'll leave a message for her now. You realize you have back-to-back meetings all day."

"Please interrupt any of my meetings when she gets here. That's all for now. Thank you, Brenda." He hadn't eaten much in the last two days and even with the hunger pains gnawing at his empty stomach, he couldn't bring himself to think about food.

Brenda strolled out of his office, her instructions to contact Kerrigan clear.

The clock on his computer read five thirty in the afternoon. Axel called Brenda back into his office. "Brenda, did you ever get in touch with Kerrigan? Where is she?"

Standing in front of his desk, Brenda fidgeted with her hands. "No sir. She hasn't returned any of my messages—voicemails, nor emails. Nothing! No one has heard from her all day, including Marie."

This was going to be harder than he thought. He was leaving that evening and would be out of town until the next week. There was little he could do besides leaving messages.

***

Friday, November 2

Axel walked through the main entrance doors to the executive suite.

Brenda gasped and brought her hand to her chest as she sucked in a hard breath. "Sir, I thought you were returning next week. Is everything okay?"

He shuffled passed her desk heading to his office, his arms overloaded with a laptop bag and duffle bag, and a small suitcase trailing behind him. "I cut my trip short. Have you heard from Kerrigan?" He yelled over his shoulder.

Hurrying from around her desk, Brenda scrambled into his office. "No sir. Not a peep. Is everything all right?" Grabbing the handle, she retrieved the small suitcase from him.

"No. Everything isn't all right. I don't know where Kerrigan is." He was losing patience, and he was beyond worry. She wasn't taking calls from him, and she wouldn't return his messages.

"Mr. Christensen, Kerrigan called out sick on Monday, but that was the last time Marie heard from her. Would you like for me to email her again?"

"No, Brenda. Call her at home again and put her through to me at once." He barked.

She sighed heavily. "Okay. I'll try her at home, again." She wheeled the suitcase next to the red leather sofa, and then exited.

Two hours later, Brenda strutted into Axel's office for a second time and stood in front of his desk. "Sir, I left another message."

He pounded his fist on the desk. "Damn! Where in the hell is she? Do you have her cell phone number?"

"No sir. I'll ask Marie for the number."

"No. No. I'll call her myself and leave another message. Please close my door. I don't want to be disturbed. Brenda, thank you."

Reaching for his cell phone, he dialed her mobile number. After, ringing several times, the call went to voicemail. Axel was beside himself now. He had only meant to jar her. She was taking their argument harder than was rational, and than he had intended. Feeling helpless, he did the only thing he could think to do. He picked up the phone and dialed the extension.

"Good afternoon, A.C. Advertising. This is Ashley Turner."

"Ashley, this is Axel Christensen. Can you come to my office now?"

She paused. "Uh, yes, yes sir. I'll be right there," she stammered.

Axel slammed down the phone and rambled his way to the door. "Brenda, Ashley Turner is on her way up. Please escort her in as soon as she arrives."

In less than five minutes, Axel swiveled around in his chair facing Ashley whose face was scrunched, her eyes narrow, and forehead wrinkled with grooves and creases. He knew Ashley would see the look of distress and anguish on his face. Bags and dark shadows settled underneath his eyes had made their semi-permanent residence.

"Brenda, please close my doors. We're not to be disturbed unless Kerrigan Mulls calls or shows up."

"Yes sir," she replied. Brenda excused herself and closed the doors.

He grimaced at Ashley. His arms waving aimlessly, "Have a seat," he said, pointing to the chairs across from his desk in one of the guest seats.

"Mr. Christensen, what's this about? How can I help you?" Ashley asked with a puzzled expression. She didn't know why she'd been summoned to meet with him.

"Ashley, please call me Axel. I need to ask you some questions. Do you mind?"

"I guess not." She paused. "What's going on?"

He leaned in closer, elbows firmly planted on top of the desk, splattered with a sea of disheveled papers. "You're friends with Kerrigan Mulls, aren't you?"

"Yes. She's my best friend. I've known her since college." Her rickety voice rang out.

"Then you know exactly what this is about, don't you?"

"I know that the two of you are involved, but no, I have no idea why you called me here today."

His hands clenched into tightly balled fists. "Ashley, I need to know that she's okay. Have you talked to her recently?"

"She hasn't returned my calls in over a week, but that's not unusual, especially since you entered the picture." Her accusatory tone didn't surprise him, and he wouldn't make any apologies.

He ran restless fingers through his dark thick mane. "I've tried calling her for the past several days and can't reach her. She called out sick on Monday, and no one has heard from her since," he muttered.

"Well, I got worried when I couldn't reach her by phone for a few days. I went to see her last Saturday afternoon. She didn't look good. She was upset and told me that the two of you had a fight, and you broke up with her. She blamed herself and defended you. I expected to see her this week, but I haven't seen her or heard from her. I only get her voicemail when I call."

He closed his eyes, taking a deep breath. "Shit! I'm sorry to bring you into this, but I'm worried. I didn't know what else to do."

He studied Ashley for a moment, and then covered his face with his hands and leaned back in his chair, groaning loudly.

"I love her so much. I didn't mean for our argument to go this far. I planned to see her Monday to work through our issues. I'll go by her place again tonight. I'm very worried. Please, if you hear from her, ask her to call me immediately."

"Mr. Christensen may I say something? What I have to say might be out of place, but she's my best friend." Her voice was confident and filled with determination.

"Go on."

"Kerrigan loves you too. She may not know how to tell you, but she does. I think you pushed too hard. You're her first relationship, and she was terrified that you'd break her heart. When you do talk to her, you need to slow things down. She needs time. You may be my boss, and I know you can fire my ass at any time, but if you hurt my friend again…"

Axel shook his head. He liked to be challenged, and he liked that Kerrigan had a good friend in Ashley. Interrupting her lecture, he filled in the blanks before she could finish. For the first time in days, a faint tease of a smile touched his arid lips. "Yes ma'am. I plan to make this right. I'm glad Kerrigan has a friend like you."

"If I hear from her, I'll ask her to call you. You're a good man. I'm glad the two of you found each other. Just fix this," Ashley quipped and stood to leave.

At that precise moment, the large oversized doors of his office flew open, slamming against the wall with a raucous bang. Brenda barreled through the doors and entered his office in a tizzy.

"Sir, I need to speak with you right away," Brenda said. He could hear the urgency in her voice.

"Ashley, thank you," he said dismissing her. He turned to Brenda as Ashley made her way out of the office and closed the doors behind her.

Brenda paced the floor, and then paused. "Mr. Christensen, I just found out that Kerrigan quit two days ago. She sent in her resignation letter to Human Resources. Marie just found out, too." She sputtered breathlessly.

"What? She quit! Why would she do that?" Axel gripped his head with both hands and threw his head back against the desk chair. "Brenda, please cancel my meetings this afternoon. I'm leaving early."

"Okay. Let me know if I can do anything to help."

He studied Brenda for a moment before speaking. He hadn't said anything about the nature of their relationship to her directly, but she had helped him plan his unofficial dates with Kerrigan and he had openly confirmed the office rumors. Of course, there had also been the time when Axel and Kerrigan made love in his office.

"Brenda, thank you. I'm sorry for being so impossible this week. I appreciate you more than you know."

"It's okay sir. I understand."

Sprinting through the building, he shoved people aside in the hallways as he dashed his way to the stairwell and then took the steps two by two on his way to his SUV parked in the garage. The odometer reached record speeds as Axel sped down the interstate. The drive to her apartment complex that would have normally taken twenty minutes only took him ten minutes. He jumped out of his vehicle and ran to her front door. Banging on the door hard, he stopped when there was no answer after several minutes. Finally, one of her neighbors emerged from across the hall.

The older man confronted him. "Is there some sort of emergency young man? You've been pounding on that door for ten minutes straight. The young lady isn't there."

"Do you know where she's gone?" he asked desperately.

"No. I think she moved out. Movers showed up yesterday."

"What! This can't be happening," he muttered under his breath. His stomach ached, as though the wind had been knocked out of him. "Thank you," he said to the man and trudged back to his vehicle, exasperated.

Axel sat there for several minutes. He had no idea why she'd done this and didn't know where she had gone. He was beside himself. Pulling out his phone, he dialed her mobile number again. This time, the phone didn't ring. Instead, the call went directly to voicemail.

"Kerrigan, this is Axel. Baby, please call me back. I'm so worried. Why did you quit? Why did you move? Where are you? We can work this out, slow things down. I'm sorry. I love you so much. I need you. I'm begging. Please call me back. Please, Kerrigan, don't do this," he pleaded.

He sat there for an hour. Finally realizing that she was gone, he drove off and went home.

CHAPTER TWELVE

Saturday, November 3

That week was the worst in Axel's life. He barely left his bedroom. Emma tried to console him, but it did little good. She was just as baffled. Though he had been harsh toward her, she had said some hurtful things to him too. Nothing seemed so severe that should have caused her to quit her job and move away. They couldn't make any sense of her actions. He was sure that she loved him as much as he loved her. The love they had shared was one-of-a-kind, and he knew there was no way she could walk away so suddenly the way she had.

Skirting along the kitchen island, Emma eased toward Axel. "Give her some time. She's hurting and scared. She'll come around," Emma said.

"It just makes no sense. Why would she move away?"

"Dear, love makes people do strange things. I'll admit, her leaving does strike me as odd, but maybe she thought you meant to end things with her. Do you think she thought you'd fire her?"

Leaning on the island, Axel buried his face in his hand. "Emma, even if she thought that, I've left message after message, apologizing for my harsh reaction. I've pleaded for her to call me. She hasn't even called back once."

Emma touched his shoulder. "Give her time. That's all you can do. Where do you think she went?" She tilted her head. Her questioning eyes meeting his anguished ones.

He threw his hands up in the air. "If I knew, I'd be there now. I have no idea. I have a few leads, which I plan to follow up on. I know her parents' names. They live in San Diego. She also has a brother who's a doctor. He also lives in San Diego. I talked with her best friend on Friday. She doesn't know anything either."

Her lips drew into a taut line across her face. "Well, if you need me, I'm here for you. Try not to worry too much. You need to rest."

Later that evening, sitting at the desk in his home office, he emailed her again.

11:49 p.m. on Saturday, November 3
To: Kerrigan Mulls
From: Axel Christensen
Subject: Worried and lonely. Please come back.
Kerrigan,
I'm sorry. Please forgive me and come back to me. I know you need time to trust me, and I need to be more patient. I want so much more with you, and sometimes it's hard for me to slow down. You mean everything to me. I love you so much. I can't imagine my life without you. Please come back. We can work through our issues together. I need you.
Always yours,
Axel

Her email bounced back. She had deleted her personal email account. Kerrigan was a ghost. He slammed his palms down on the desk. A sharp pain shot up and recoiled through his arms. He screamed into the stillness of the room, his heartache much more severe than any physical pain. His plan had backfired in the worst imaginable way.

***

Wednesday, December 19

Nearly two months had passed since Kerrigan's disappearing act. Axel hadn't been the same since. He was withdrawn and sullen. He poured all his effort into his work, and into finding her. He had been traveling quite a bit for work, slowing down the progress on his search for her. The month prior, he had hired a private investigator, Michael Jones, who up to this point hadn't been able to find anything substantial on her. There weren't even any leads on Facebook or any other social networking sites. She had dropped off the face of the earth. Jones had given him the last known address and phone number for her parents. He had written a letter addressed to her there, but the envelope was returned as undeliverable. He had also tried calling their last known phone number, but that number had been disconnected with no forwarding number. His last resort was to track down her brother Jordan, a doctor in the San Diego area, and that fact made tracking him down easy. He had anticipated that Jordan would protect his sister, but he hoped he would be objective and perhaps even willing to help once he explained the situation.

***

Kerrigan had cut all ties with her friends, including Ashley. Her decision wasn't personal, but she didn't want to be reminded of that life. The wound hurt too much. The memory of the day she discovered the truth about Axel was still so fresh as if she walked into the coffee shop yesterday. She was too embarrassed and hurt to tell anyone what she had heard him say about her, what he had done to her. She decided to start over anew and forget her time in Atlanta. She was in survival mode, retreating home to San Diego was all she knew to do.

Kerrigan rested in his home office on the sofa sobbing her heart out.

She lie across the sofa, her feet propped up on the armrest, and her head snuggled into an emerald green throw pillow at the other end. "I've been sick since I left the East Coast. I just can't shake this nauseous feeling, and the daily headaches are killing me."

Jordan, who sat in the window seat opposite her, lifted his head. "Little sis, maybe you should go see a doctor. Do you have any other symptoms?"

She leaned up on her elbow. "You're always on the clock." Her scowl turned in a slight grin. "I never knew heartbreak would take such a physical toll on me. I haven't been able to eat or sleep, and I'm sure the lack of food and rest, have made my symptoms worse."

Jordan stood, ambled to the sofa and sat next to her feet. "As a doctor, but more importantly as your overly protective big brother, I really think you should see someone. It might be nothing—heartbreak as you said. But as a precaution, you should be checked out." He stood again and headed to his desk. Opening the top drawer, he retrieved a stack of business cards and riffled through them. "Here, take this."

She snatched the card from him. "You do realize we live in the era of smartphones, don't you? You could've texted the number to me." She teased.

Scrunching his nose just the way their father did whenever he was being firm, Jordan frowned. "I mean what I said, Kerrigan. Call tomorrow and make an appointment."

"Relax, will you? I'll make an appointment."

***

Kerrigan twisted her hands in her lap, her eyes darting over the charts and posters that hung on the pale yellow walls of the sterile room. Jordan had recommended Dr. Sanders. The ill feeling she had for the past few weeks had worsened in a week. The nausea turned to vomiting, and bouts of sickness, increased every day.

Dr. Sanders was a petite middle-aged woman who resembled an Irish pixie with her upturned nose and pointy ears. The minutes passed and seemed like hours. She was taking too long to return. Something must have been wrong. Finally, Dr. Sanders entered the room with her paperwork and lab results in hand. She was restless as Dr. Sanders pulled out the lab work and scanned it over.

She wore a gentle smile. "Kerrigan, I have your results. Are you ready?"

"Yes. Is everything okay?"

"Well, that depends."

Suddenly, she gulped hard, and the walls were spinning around Kerrigan, fast. She clung to the sides of the examination table to keep from falling off.

"Depends on what? What does it say?"

"Congratulations. You're pregnant. We'll do an ultrasound, but from what you've told me, my guess is that you're about eight to ten weeks along."

"Pregnant? How's that possible? I mean, I know how babies are made, but I was a virgin up until two months ago. I didn't think it could happen so fast, especially since I'm on birth control."

Doctor Sanders took her hand. "You've been having unprotected sex. You said you were on birth control?"

"Yes, I was taking them to regulate my cycle."

"Have you missed any pills?"

"No … I don't remember. I don't think so. Maybe once." She recalled forgetting the pill the day of their argument, and perhaps a couple of other times. "I didn't think skipping a few pills would matter."

"Skipping pills increases your odds of getting pregnant. There's no denying this. The baby is real, but you have options if this isn't what you want."

She wrapped her arms around her belly, and winced. "You mean abortion? I couldn't do that."

"That's one option, but that's not your only choice. There's also adoption."

"Dr. Sanders, I couldn't do that either."

"Then the only other option is to have this baby, and love and care for your child."

She leaned forward and sobbed softly, then pulled her arms even tighter around her body. Her life had taken an unexpected turn, yet again. This was the cruelest twist of fate. There was no escaping the memory of Axel Christensen.

"Thank you, Dr. Sanders. I'll think over my options, but the facts are that I can't afford a baby right now. I have no job, no insurance and I'm living with my brother until I land on my feet again. I hadn't planned on a baby, especially right now."

"This is none of my business, and you don't have to answer, but maybe something for you to consider. Perhaps the baby's father would be willing to help."

Tears welled up in Kerrigan's eyes again, a different sort of sickness invaded her stomach.

"Thanks. I'll think it over." There was no way she would involve Axel. He didn't want anything to do with her, and a child was the last thing he wanted.

Dr. Sanders grabbed her other hand, squeezed and then released it. She handed her some tissues and informational pamphlets. "Here are some resources to help you with your decision. Whatever you do, make sure you can live with your choice. I suggest you speak to a professional who can help you think through the best decision for you."

***

Seated at the ornately carved dining room table with Jordan and his wife Nicole, Kerrigan was haunted by her news. She barely paid attention to the casual conversation at the table.

Jordan faced her with concern in his eyes. "You seem distracted this evening. Is everything okay?" Jordan's brows pressed together. "How did the appointment go today?"

Kerrigan closed her eyes and hung her head. "Well, I know what's wrong with me." Lifting her head, she eyed Jordan, and then Nicole, with tears in her eyes. "I'm pregnant," she muttered softly.

Jordan stilled, glanced at Nicole and then brought his hand to his chin. He stared at Kerrigan in silence before speaking. "I suspected you might be. The cottage has plenty of room, a small kitchen, living area, a bathroom. Stay as long as you like."

He and Nicole had a beautiful six-bedroom home, and the quaint guest cottage was a bonus that would be enough space for her and the baby.

"I don't want to intrude. I'm barely showing, so it should be easy for me to get a job. I'll start paying rent and then I'll look for my own place. I have a few good job leads."

Nicole touched her hand. "Don't worry about a thing. We only use that cottage for out of town guests, and you're the only one who ever visits."

"Kerrigan, you're single, you have no job, and you have a baby on the way. Now is not the time to be stubborn. Family takes care of each other. Being a single mother isn't going to be easy. You're staying." Jordan chastised her the way he did when she was his twelve-year-old sister and he was the older adult brother.

"Thank you both for taking me in." Her emotional state teetered on the edge of tears.

He frowned. "Does the father know? You haven't said anything about him." Jordan asked, his curiosity and concern piqued.

"No. I will take care of my baby. He doesn't need to know."

"Are you sure? I think you should at least consider giving him the option. If it were me, I'd want to know."

"Believe me. Axel isn't interested. Can we drop this?"

That was as much as she planned on saying about Axel Christensen.

***

Friday, December 21

He sat staring blankly at the computer monitor on his desk. Where is she? Two months had gone by, and he hadn't heard one word from her. The realization that he may never hear from her or see her again was slowly killing him inside. As though he had willed it to happen, the phone rang, jarring him back to life.

Slumping over his desk, he reached for it. "Axel Christensen." He answered with a lifeless drone.

"Axel, this is Jones. I have good news for you. I found her."

He perked up, sat straight up in his chair and stilled. "Where is she? Is she okay?" His voice was excited and anxious.

"She's in San Diego. I think she's living with her brother Dr. Jordan Mulls. Take down these two phone numbers. One is Dr. Mulls' cell phone number, and the other is the number at his residence. I also have an address, but I wouldn't go knocking on the door just yet if I were you. You need to establish contact first. Maybe try reaching out to her brother."

"Jones, thank you. I'll give him a call now."

"Slow down. I know you're eager, but there's the time-zone difference to take into consideration. It's six thirty in the morning, in San Diego."

"You're right. I'm anxious. I don't want to lose track of her again. I'll wait until eight o'clock, their time." He blew out a hard breath.

***

Precisely at eight o'clock, he dialed the number Jones had given him to reach Dr. Mulls. The phone had rung five times before Jordan answered.

"Hello, this is Dr. Mulls."

"Hi, Dr. Mulls. You don't know me, but my name is Axel Christensen. I know this is going to sound bizarre, but I'm a desperate man." He paused and took a deep breath. "I was involved with your sister before she moved back to San Diego. She worked for my company. I'm not sure if she's ever mentioned me." There was a long pause before Axel continued. "We had an argument, and she left town suddenly without giving word to me or anyone here." Axel's hands were clammy and his heart hammered in his chest. "I don't know what happened. I've been trying to find her, to talk things over. Things were going well between us, and then she just disappeared. I've been trying to find her for almost two months. I just want to talk to her. I understand she's living with you. Is she okay?"

Jordan recognized Axel's name. "I don't know how you got this number, but I'm sorry, I can't help you."

Axel paced the length of the office, his loafers clicking across the hardwood. "Dr. Mulls, please hear me out. I'm a decent person. I love your sister, and I would never do anything to harm her. I need to know what happened, why she left. You may not want to hear this, but I'm going insane without her." The perpetual knot in his gut twisted as he pled his case. "You're married, right? Do you remember the feeling you had when you knew your wife was the one? What if she up and left without any explanation, no goodbye, nothing? Kerrigan was the first and only woman I've ever loved. I thought I was going to spend my life with her. I just don't understand what happened. One day she was here, and the next day she had disappeared. I've been so worried and confused." Sadness and sorrow resonated in his words, and he didn't care that the sound of desperation leaked from his lips.

"Mr. Christensen, I hear your pain. I don't know what happened between the two of you. She hasn't talked to me about your relationship in detail. All she said was that you hurt her deeply. She's doing well. I suggest you move on."

"Dr. Mulls, I'm a desperate man. I can't move on until I know what I did, why she left. I'm unsettled. We got into an argument because I wanted to take our relationship to the next level and she wasn't ready—she was insecure." He moved to the bookcase where he had placed three framed photos of Kerrigan. Tears built behind Axel's eyes and his voice wavered. "I know I was putting too much pressure on her, but the whole situation is mind boggling how she suddenly quit her job and moved across the country days after an argument. I need closure at least."

"You don't know what caused her to leave?"

"Not at all—one minute we were in love and the next minute she was gone. If I knew what I had done, I wouldn't be so confused. I was planning to propose to her the day of our fight so you can imagine my heartache."

"I have an idea, but I'm not making any promises. I'll try to talk with her tonight. If I learn anything, I'll call you back. You realize that I shouldn't be helping you."

"I know this is awkward, but I do appreciate your help. Can you at least tell me how she's doing? Is she okay? I want to know that she's okay."

"She's having ... a rough patch, but she'll be okay." He heard the hesitation in Jordan's voice.

"Please let me know if she needs anything. I can send money, whatever she needs. She doesn't have to know it's from me."

"You sound like a generous and reasonable man. I can tell you care for her. I'll call you back this evening. You're three hours ahead. Should I call you in the morning instead?"

"No. Please call this evening, anytime. I'll be waiting. I can't thank you enough, Dr. Mulls."

***

That evening after dinner, Jordan asked Kerrigan to join him in his study. The two disappeared into the office, and Jordan motioned for her to sit next to him on the sofa.

"How are you feeling little sis?"

"I'm exhausted. I can't wait for this stage to pass."

"You'll feel better soon." He touched her arm. "I've been meaning to talk to you about something that's bothering me. I'd like to know about this Axel fellow. What happened between you two?"

She sank deep into the sofa. "I thought he loved me." She looked down and away from Jordan. "He said and did all the right things in the beginning, but he was moving too fast for me, and it scared me."

"So, that's why you left him? Because he was moving too fast and you were scared off?" he asked.

"No. There's more. We had a horrible argument one morning, and he stormed out on me. Later that day, I stopped at a coffee shop on my way to his house to apologize. He was there with another woman. They didn't see me, but I saw them and overheard their conversation."

Her voice trembled, and her eyes filled with tears. "I heard him tell the woman that he had used me, gotten what he wanted and that he was done with me. I worked for his company, and I couldn't stand the embarrassment I'd face if I went back to work." She glanced at the wall clock hanging over his desk, wondering how long Jordan's interrogation would last.

She sobbed a little. "Some of my co-workers had already begun rumors before our relationship was public knowledge. I hated every minute. He confronted one of the leading culprits and announced to everyone in the department that we were involved." She stared blankly across the room at nothing in particular. Tears streamed down Kerrigan's face, the room melted into a blur of colors and shapes. "I couldn't face the ridicule of that mob, especially after what I had heard. He's a wealthy man. I knew he was a player. He told me that he loved me—that he wanted to spend his life with me. I allowed myself to believe his lies. I should have known better."

Jordan pondered her explanation. "Did you ever confront him about what you saw and overheard or tell him why you left?"

"No. I didn't see the point."

"I understand how you feel, but are you sure you have the whole story? Is it possible that you misunderstood what you heard?"

Her face heated. "Jordan, why are you taking his side? I know what I heard. There were no mistaking Axel's words. He called me a slut and said he got what he wanted. He said he wished I'd disappear. So I did."

Jordan folded his arms across his chest. "I'm not taking sides. I'm concerned for you. You're having this man's baby. Regardless of what happened, I think you have to tell him. Besides, he should be responsible to help you care for the child."

"Jordan, I believed he loved me. Our whole relationship was a lie. He betrayed my trust. I can't face him. I can't talk to him. He hurt me too badly. I will find a way to care for my child without Axel Christensen. I don't want a damn thing from him."

Sitting on the desk across from them, his cell phone vibrated, thudding against the wood. "I understand how you feel." Jordan stood and hurried to the phone. "But, as your big brother, my job is to be concerned about you. Go get some rest. I'm on call this evening. Looks as if I'm being called in."

"Thanks, Jordan. I'll be fine. You know I'm a fighter." Rising from the sofa, she made her way to the doorway. He grabbed his coat from the coat rack and his brief case from the side of his desk. Kerrigan trailed him as he rushed to the garage.

He pulled his Lexus onto the road and the car disappeared out of sight. She didn't know what she would have done without her brother. She wrapped her arms around her belly, a faint smile forming across lips that had been forced into a frown for so long that she wasn't sure she'd ever smile again. He could be annoying, but she was grateful for Jordan's protective nature.

***

Axel answered on the second ring. The phone had become an appendage, as vital as his lungs were to breathing air. "Dr. Mulls, I'm so grateful you called back. Did you learn anything?" He sat at the edge of the bed, his palms suddenly moistening.

"I learned a lot, actually. You used my sister. Who's the woman Kerrigan saw you with?"

Words were a prisoner in Axel's parched throat. A bottle of tepid water at his bedside freed his trapped sentences. "I didn't use Kerrigan. I love her." His temperature rose one hundred degrees or he had just entered hell. "What woman are you talking about because I have no idea? I didn't date anyone for almost year before being with Kerrigan and I haven't seen anyone since she left me." Axel rose and paced the room with a frantic stride.

"Then you must have a twin brother because she saw you with another woman." Jordan's sarcasm bled into his ears making him flinch and yank the phone away. He stared at the thing as if he could melt the device with his vision.

Flush with anger, he brought the phone back to his ear. "Saw me where? When? I swear since the day Kerrigan walked into my office, she's the only woman I've wanted, dated. I don't know what on earth she thinks she saw." His voice raised several octaves.

"Well, she didn't just see you with another woman—she heard your conversation with this woman. You said that you had gotten what you wanted from her—that you were done with her." Axel's mind raced at Jordan's accusation, and his chest pounded. "You called my sister a slut and said you wished she'd disappear. She heard the words come out of your mouth, Mr. Christensen." Silence fell between them.

Axel's heart sank. He thought back to his conversation with Melody months ago. He recalled from memory the words he'd spoken. I'm done with her now. I got what I wanted. She's history to me. I wouldn't care if she dropped off the face of the earth. In fact, I wish that slut would disappear. He fell into his bedside chair, and slumped as a chill raced up his spine.

Angry that he had allowed his temper to flare and had spoken such awful things in a fit of rage, he closed his eyes and stilled. Why didn't she confront him? Instead, she ran away. Axel pushed himself to his feet again, walking over to his bar. Bottled water wouldn't suffice.

Amber liquid filled the glass, nearing the rim. Lifted to thin lips, he swigged down the shot of bourbon, his liquid fortitude. The glass went down on the bar with a gentle tap. "Dr. Mulls, it's true, I said some very ugly things." Despite his fury, Axel kept his voice even. "The woman Kerrigan saw me talking to is my cousin Melody. We were discussing my ongoing lawsuit against a woman named Sara Murphy. I told Kerrigan about Sara, but I never disclosed details about the case." Axel's body tensed.

Forced from the shadows, he had to talk about the dark secret that he managed to keep hidden from the world. "After ten long years, I had finally won my lawsuit against Sara for defamation of character and a litany of other charges. What's your email address? I'd like to send you links to some articles that will help explain the whole story." He sat back down in the chair, resting his elbows on his knees and leaning forward. "This, this …" His stomach tightened, and he clenched a fist. "This scandal had been a giant source of pain in my life, and I was finally done with it. Melody and I were celebrating. The horrible things I said were about Sara, not Kerrigan."

Jordan didn't rebuttal. Instead, he gave his email address. "I'm at the hospital now. I may get called into surgery. Give me a minute. I'm trying to skim over your email on my cell phone."

Nervous waves drummed through Axel's body as time passed while Jordan read the articles.

"Mr. Christensen, I don't know what to say." He paused. "You need to see her and explain things in person."

His pulse raced. "Please call me Axel. Will you help me Dr. Mulls? I want to fix things between us." For the first time since Kerrigan left, the weight he carried lightened.

"Call me Jordan. When can you be in San Diego?"

"In two weeks. I'm going out of the country on business tomorrow morning. I'd be heading to San Diego right now if that were possible."

"You really love her, don't you?"

"Yes, I do. Please don't say anything to her. I want to surprise her."

"You have my word."

His heart swelled. "Thank you, Jordan." He had reason for hope.

***

They hung up. Renewed energy washed over him. Jordan had discovered the reason for her abrupt return to San Diego. Axel leaped up from his chair, anxious, unable to sleep, and filled with anxiety. He wanted to cancel his trip and see her immediately, but he couldn't. Six business clients would be affected. He knew he would be distracted throughout his trip, thinking about her the entire time. He was determined to return a week early. He composed an email to Brenda, requesting she send a gift basket to Jordan's office thanking him for his help. He also instructed her to make seven-day accommodations at one of the best five star hotels in San Diego. The next two weeks would be hell, but he hoped the pay-off would be worth the torture.

CHAPTER THIRTEEN

Monday, December 24

Kerrigan could feel her belly getting harder and rounder now. She was just over ten weeks pregnant. The daily dash to the nearest toilet or trash bin to release the contents of her stomach was getting better day by day. Telling her parents about her pregnancy had been one of the most difficult things she had ever done. Although she was twenty-nine years old, they were disappointed and worried about her being a single parent. She joined her mother for lunch one afternoon to talk about her predicament.

Now that she was responsible for the little life growing inside her, she was extra careful about what she ate. Kerrigan was glad that her mother had suggested a restaurant that served fresh organic meals. They were seated in a booth along the wall and sunlight flickering through the shaded window cast bands of glowing amber across her face. The lanky waiter strolled over to their table introduced himself as Jeff, and took their drink orders. She had counted the minutes before her mother tore into her. Eight.

"Kerrigan, I know you've said that you don't want anything to do with the baby's father, but you ought to at least ask him to help you. Children are expensive." Her mother's graceful piano fingers unfolded the napkin and laid the cloth across her lap. "Your father and I struggled for many years, and there were two of us in the household."

"Mom, I know this will be hard, but I can do it on my own. My new job at the boutique doesn't pay as well as the job in Atlanta, but the work will keep me occupied and provide enough income for rent and basic needs." She had already purchased a few items including a crib from the boutique where she worked. Each week, she purchased new things. "Besides, I haven't told him. I can't deal with him right now." The mere thought of talking to Axel gave her palpitations.

Her mother eyed Jeff as he placed two glasses of water on the table. "Honey, I understand that you're hurting." She made sure he was out of earshot before continuing. "You may not want to face or deal with whatever happened between the two of you, but you need to think about your child ahead of yourself. You have to tell him. He has a right to know about his child. He may surprise you and offer to help."

Kerrigan pushed back from the table, sinking deeper into the booth's plush leather seat. "I'm not involving him, and that's that." *Why couldn't her family respect what she wanted?*

"You sound pretty angry and hurt. Do you want to tell me about what happened?"

She rolled her eyes and huffed. "Not in particular. The fact that I'm pregnant should spell everything out for you. I was naïve and stupid. He simply wanted sex. I thought he cared about me, but he was only using me. I'm knocked up. There's nothing else to tell." Grabbing the glass with two hands wishing it were potent enough to drown her troubles, she brought her lips to the rim and gulped.

Her mother raised her brow and pursed her lips. "What does he do for a living?" she asked, staring a hole through Kerrigan.

Outside on the patio, a man and a little girl sat a table alone. Turning away, her eyes met her mother's imposing stare. "He was my boss. He owns the company where I worked." The thought of Axel playing any part in her child's life like the man outside made tears well up.

"Are you talking about the man with the odd name? Then surely he can help provide for your child." She raised her hands in the air.

She greedily gulped her water. "Mom, please. I don't want to talk about Axel. I was incredibly stupid to get involved with him. I should have known better. People like him don't get involved with ordinary people like me. I'm trying to move on. I don't want anything to do with him." Her hands trembled, and she could feel her face warm.

"What do you mean people like him don't get involved with ordinary people like you? Kerrigan, you're beautiful and intelligent. That's his problem if he doesn't recognize what a gift you are. Honey, are you still in love with him?" her mother asked, placing a hand on Kerrigan's forearm.

"Mom," Kerrigan huffed, and then she turned away, her gaze back to the man and child outside. "Yes, I love him, but it was foolish of me to get involved and to give away my heart to him. It was dumb of me to think he loved me back. He comes from a different world than mine. I was an experiment to him. Now, can we drop the subject? I don't want to talk about him." Eyes heavy with moisture, she wiped the burgeoning tears away. Black smudges stained her white napkin with a swirl of squiggly shapes from mascara that rubbed off.

"Okay honey. I'm sorry I upset you. Your dad and I are worried about you and our unborn grandchild. We just want what's best for you." She leaned over the table and tapped the tip of Kerrigan's nose the way she had always done since Kerrigan was old enough to remember. "You know that we'll support you in your decision. We'll do whatever we can do to help."

Her mother had a way of making her feel as if she was a little girl safe under the protection of doting parents.

Taut lips relaxed, a spontaneous rise at the corners of her mouth was a wavering smile as stark as the smudges of stained mascara smeared on her white napkin. "I hadn't planned on being a single mother, but I'll be okay. The baby will be okay, too. Somehow, I'll figure it all out." She closed her eyes. If only she could believe her own words—that everything would all work out in the end.

***

Wednesday, December 26

Kerrigan had changed everything in her life when she moved back to San Diego. The way she had left things with Ashley was bad. Before she canceled her email account, she had sent Ashley a message to say that she would be in contact once she was settled. Now that she was pregnant, she had been reluctant to reach out, afraid that Ashley might say something about the baby to Axel. Everyone seemed to be siding with him, saying he had a right to know. Instead, she decided to mail a short letter to Ashley.

Ash,

I miss you so much. I hope you're okay. I'm sorry I left the way I did without saying goodbye. I'll explain everything to you one day. I think you'll understand. My life has taken on some unexpected twists and turns, and I've certainly been better than I am now, but I know I'll get through the challenges ahead of me. I'm still trying to get myself settled in my new home and life. I found a job working at a small boutique. The pay isn't great, but I like my co-workers, and along with my savings, I can pay the bills. I'm learning the ins and outs of running a small boutique. You know that's always been my dream. Please don't let Axel know that you heard from me. That chapter in my life is over, and I'm trying to move on peacefully. I'll write again soon.

Kerri

***

Friday, December 28

The wheels on the plane extended, beginning its initial descent into San Diego International Airport. Axel's growth and expansion plans had suffered already—his lack of focus over the past weeks was to blame—and cutting his business trip short wasn't going to make much of a difference. He arrived in San Diego a week early. Jordan would be waiting at the airport, to take him to Loews Coronado Bay Resort, where Brenda had made reservations for his stay.

Axel emerged from the airport, his eyes searching for Jordan's silver Lexus among a sea of cars and trucks and transportation shuttles. A car matching the description Jordan had given pulled up to the curb. The stately man inside dressed in scrubs carefully scanned passersby as though he was trying to identify his would-be passenger. Axel strode over cautiously. The passenger window lowered.

Leaning down, he poked his head through the narrow opening. "Jordan?" Axel reached inside and extended his hand.

A steady hand met Axel's firm grip. "Good to meet you Axel. Put your luggage in the trunk and hop in." Jordan pressed a button releasing the trunk. Slowly, the bonnet glided up.

Axel eyed the meticulously laundered suit hanging in the vehicle's rear. "Nice to meet you too, although I do wish we were meeting under different circumstances." Jordan nodded.

Skirting a large man wheeling a cart of assorted luggage, Axel made his way to the trunk and tossed his bags inside. Sauntering back to the door, he climbed inside and sank into the passenger seat.

"How was the redeye?" Jordan asked.

Axel raised his brow. "Too early and too long, but it's the most important trip I'll ever take. Thank you for the ride."

"Not a problem."

"Jordan, I can't thank you enough for your help with everything." He tugged at his collar and twisted his neck, giving Jordan a sidelong glance.

Jordan guided the car away from the curb. "I just hope you can make things right with my sister. I know you care for her." He glanced at Axel, and then returned his focus to the road.

Tearing his eyes from the majestic view of the bright blue sky and tall palms, Axel faced Jordan. "I love her—I'm in love with her." For the first time, he understood what it meant to love someone. "I didn't come all the way to San Diego to screw this up. I need your help with something else. I would like to speak with your parents. Would it be possible for me to talk to them today?"

Jordan eyed him tentatively. "I'll help you, but let's take this one step at a time. Do you have a plan?"

Axel smiled and gave an affirmative nod. "Yes, the ball is already in motion. Now, I just need to think through what I'll say to her."

"I think I can arrange for you to speak with my parents later today. Kerrigan said you moved quickly, she wasn't kidding." Jordan chuckled.

He rested his head against the seat. "I love your sister, and she loves me too. I'm a man who knows what he wants. I see no reason to procrastinate or delay the inevitable."

"I can't believe how calm you are," Jordan remarked.

"Calm? I'm nervous like hell, but what Kerrigan and I share…" He paused, and then focused his gaze out the window, peering at the open sea. "I've never been more certain about anything in my life."

The drive to the resort took under an hour, and the scenic view along North Harbor Drive was breathtaking.

Surrounded by the splendor and beauty of the resort, the car came to a halt at the hotel's unloading area.

Jordan faced Axel. "I'll call you later about the meeting with my parents. If you need anything, give me a call. You have my mobile number."

Axel nodded and moved his hand to the door handle. "Thank you for everything, Jordan." He opened the door, shook Jordan's hand again and exited the car. "See you later today."

After checking in, he made his way to his suite to unpack, and then went to pick up the rental car that was reserved for him.

Anxious to get to Kerrigan, Axel jogged pass customers and lot attendants on his way to his rental car. Seated, buckled in and ready to go, he pulled out his GPS, his hurried fingers hammering in the address where Kerrigan worked. Armed with information that Jordan had shared, she would be arriving at work soon. Thirty minutes later, he turned into the lot, parked the car near the boutique and jumped out.

Spotting a coffee shop, he decided to grab some coffee while working through his plan and his nerves. He needed to think through his next moves carefully.

***

Kerrigan awoke refreshed and feeling better physically than she had in weeks. She was nearing the end of her first trimester. Today, she decided to wear a blue dress. Her clothes had begun to fit snugly around her mid-section, her little round belly now starting to show. She planned to go shopping for maternity clothes that weekend.

That morning before going to work, she made her usual rounds—a quick stop for a small coffee and a brisk walk to the boutique where she worked. The white sweater she wore would stave off the morning chill. Rounding the sidewalk's curve, she strolled to the door.

***

In walked Kerrigan. Her gait graceful, she floated across the floor. Axel's heart nearly stopped when he laid eyes on her. With her hair piled on top of her head, delicate wavy tendrils cascaded the nape of her neck and teased her temples. She was gorgeous, even more beautiful than he remembered, radiant. Seeing her and hearing her melodic voice as she ordered sent a wave of nerves through him so fierce that the wind was knocked out of him. As if on command, his cock stiffened. She didn't recognize him sitting at the table near the window wearing a white baseball cap and sunglasses.

Axel raised the newspaper high, hiding his face. Listening to the light banter between her and the man at the counter, she was a regular customer. It took everything in his being not to jump up and take her into his arms. In that instant, he had the clarity he needed, and he knew what he would do and say to her. Peering over his paper, his wide eyes followed the sway of her hips as she left and strolled down the sidewalk until she disappeared from view.

***

When she walked in at nine o'clock, the quaint boutique was abuzz, which was unusual since traffic didn't pick up until ten o'clock or later. She didn't know what all the commotion was about when Sandy, the owner came barreling toward her.

Kerrigan stripped her white sweater away.

She yelled across the store to Kerrigan. "You look exceptionally beautiful and pregnant this morning." The skinny, blonde cheerleader-type had the energy and gumption twice that of most forty-something-year-olds. "You have an admirer who thinks so too."

Kerrigan frowned. "Sandy, what on earth are you talking about?"

An index finger pointed toward the front counter. "Take a look, these beautiful roses came for you a few minutes ago." Sandy grinned. "You've been holding out on us. We're dying to know who sent them."

Kerrigan gasped, her jaw dropped. She cupped her mouth with her hand. She had only received flowers like those from one person in her life, Axel Christensen. The fragrant smell of fresh roses filled the air. She walked over to the beautiful arrangement and inhaled. The note attached was short, not giving much away.

Beautiful roses, for a beautiful woman with a beautiful soul.

Always and forever,

Yours

She thought of Axel again. The expression and sentiment sounded very much like him, and her stomach knotted with anxiety. She read the signature again. *Yours.* That was Axel's signature.

Tears filled her eyes. Kerrigan recalled the love she believed they shared. "Sandy, there must be some mistake with the delivery. These flowers can't be for me. They must be for someone else. I don't know anyone who would send those flowers to me."

"Well, you're wrong because somebody did, you lucky girl," Sandy said.

The ruckus in the boutique died down, and everyone went back to his or her tasks. Her job was to greet and assist customers with their selections. Since new items came in daily, she also helped display many of the new products. She unpacked the boxes that Sandy had given her. One box contained a perfect, handmade blanket. She fell in love with the soft fabric, but the price tag was well over her budget. All morning, she kept eyeing the blanket. Finally, she decided to mention the blanket to Sandy.

"Sandy, would you consider putting this blanket aside? The blanket is perfect, but I need a couple of weeks to save up. I'm allowing myself one splurge item for the baby."

"Consider the blanket a gift from me. Put it away behind the counter and save your money for something else. This gift is the least I can do after your help."

"Oh Sandy, that's so generous of you. Thank you!"

Kerrigan's smile spanned her entire face. She folded the blanket and placed it into a bag, carefully tucking the generous gift behind the counter.

The rest of the day went on like any typical day. She organized items on the shelves and assisted customers with their purchases. The store was large and when busy, keeping track of all the customers was sometimes difficult, but the pace made her day entertaining. Today was no exception. There were three conferences happening in town and they were busier than they'd ever been.

"Kerrigan, you're brilliant. I think we're going to reach record sales today, thanks to you," Sandy said.

Kerrigan was glad that the marketing plan she created for Sandy was already showing positive results. Patrons from participating hospitality businesses flocked to receive their discount and complimentary gift.

"I'm glad I was able to put my marketing savvy to use. I have some other ideas, too." She patted the woman on the arm.

She was glad she had found Sandy and the boutique. This was what she had always wanted to do, and she needed the diversion from her life.

CHAPTER FOURTEEN

Axel drove to the address Jordan had given him to meet at his parents' house at noon. He waited in the vehicle until he saw Jordan approaching. He bounded out of the car and joined him. The two men shook hands and walked toward the house. Jordan had told Axel that he purchased the home for Mr. and Mrs. Mulls years earlier after a fire had destroyed the apartment building where they lived. It explained why his previous attempts to reach them had failed.

Jordan knocked, and a beautiful older woman appeared at the door. After peeking through the sidelight windows and seeing them standing on the porch, she opened the door.

"Jordan! My favorite handsome son. We haven't seen you in weeks. How are Nicole and the girls?" she asked, motioning the men inside the house.

"Mom, you know I'm always on call. Nicole and the girls are fine, the same as the last time you saw them, Saturday, right?" He smiled.

She opened her arms and drew him in. Axel studied her carefully, taken aback. Mrs. Mulls was a strikingly beautiful woman. She looked like Kerrigan, just mature. Kerrigan had inherited her mother's delicate features and graceful curvy frame.

Jordan's father joined the three of them in the foyer.

"Mom and dad, this is Axel Christensen, Kerrigan's boyfriend. He's come all the way to San Diego to clarify the misunderstanding that caused their breakup. He's explained everything to me. I believe he's a good man. Kerrigan doesn't know he's here yet. He'll surprise her later today, but he wanted to talk to you first about his intentions."

***

Mr. Mulls glared at him, an unforgiving scowl his eyes protruded, and nostrils flared. He flexed his hands and cracked his knuckles.

"Mr. Mulls, it's a pleasure to meet you. Kerrigan always speaks so fondly of you both," Axel said, extending his clammy hand, nervous eyes dancing between Mr. and Mrs. Mulls.

Eyeing him up and down, and strutting like a peacock, Mr. Mulls puffed out his chest, and then glared. His hands resting at his side didn't budge.

Mrs. Mulled stepped between the men. She reached out a delicate hand to Axel. "Axel, I'm Kerrigan's mother. Come on in. We'll sit in the living room."

Axel's eyes shifted between her and Mr. Mulls' cold glare. "Thank you, ma'am. Good to meet you both."

"I'd like to know exactly what happened between you and my daughter. I'll make up my mind about you then." Mr. Mulls said, his sour face contorted.

Walking into the living room, Axel's eyes floated around the room. His gaze landed on an upright piano, the top covered with trophies and picture frames. Stepping closer, he recognized Kerrigan's smile in most of the photographs and her name was etched into the gold-tone nameplate on all of the trophies.

Mrs. Mulls paused beside him. "Kerrigan plays beautifully. Did she ever play for you?"

Remembering the first time she played for him brought sensual memories back. "Yes, she played for me once." His pulse quickened at the thought. “You have an exceptionally talented daughter. She plays beautifully.” He missed holding her, and he couldn’t wait to have her in his arms again.

Mrs. Mulls stared into him. “She could have gone so much further with her music, but she simply stopped playing.” She shook her head, blankly staring across the room. “She could have done so much more with her life.”

Axel pressed his eyebrows together, frowning. “Mrs. Mulls, Kerrigan is a very accomplished woman. You should be proud of her. I believe she can do anything she sets her mind to.”

Pursing her lips, she grabbed the back of her neck. “I agree, but that was before the…” She snapped her head around and faced him. “Never mind. Please have a seat. I’m heading to the kitchen for refreshments and drinks. I’ll be right back.”

Axel joined the other two men in the living room. He sat across from Mr. Mulls who idled in a worn recliner. While she was gone, Jordan and Axel chatted casually about sports. Mr. Mulls sat back silently, his glare locked on Axel. As soon as she entered the room, Mrs. Mulls kicked off the interrogation in blunt fashion.

“Axel, what happened? Kerrigan has admitted to me that she loves you. Why did she quit her job and move all the way back to San Diego? She loved her job, her life and you.”

He told them the entire sorted story, starting with Sara—how she had tried extorting money from him and this family with her lies about him allegedly raping her when the two were in college.

Leaning forward with his forearms resting on his thighs, he spoke softly. “After Sara, I was devastated. Mr. and Mrs. Mulls, Kerrigan is my first serious relationship.” He hung his head down. “I loved her—I am in love with her. I was ready to take our relationship to the next level, but she was insecure and doubted my feelings for her. I don’t understand.” His baritone quivered, and then heat rose to his face as nerves were getting the best of Axel.

Mrs. Mulls patted his shoulder. "Yes, Kerrigan expressed her insecurity about your relationship to me too. I don't understand either."

Axel lifted himself and addressed Mr. Mulls directly. "We had an argument. That was the last time I saw her, more than two months ago. I was shocked to learn the next week after our argument that she had quit and moved away. Until I talked to Jordan, I had no idea what happened."

She pivoted in her seat to the left. "Jordan, did Kerrigan say why she left?" Mrs. Mulls asked.

"Kerrigan saw and overheard Axel talking to a woman in a coffee shop. It was a misunderstanding. She heard him making disparaging remarks, and she thought he'd been talking about her when he had been talking about Sara."

The boom of voice caught their attention. "Who was the woman you were talking to?" Mr. Mulls asked.

"The woman she saw me talking to is my cousin Melody. I had just won my lawsuit against Sara. Melody has been my confidant over the years. We've been close since childhood. I'd been spending most of my time with Kerrigan. When we greeted each other that day in the coffee shop Melody asked me why she hadn't seen much of me. I responded with one word—Kerrigan." He took as deep breath, assessing the Mulls' reaction to his story.

Mrs. Mulls leaned in close, her eyes narrowed and focused on his as he spoke.

Continuing his explanation, "I hadn't dated anyone seriously since the incident with Sara until I met your daughter. Melody said she was glad that I was finally moving on. I shifted our conversation and unloaded about Sara."

Axel glanced at Mr. Mulls and noted his brow drawn down; his expression hard like chiseled stone.

Mr. Mulls shifted in his seat and then cracked his knuckles. "Did Kerrigan ever tell you I was in the Army?"

"Yes sir. She did." A light coat of sweat glazed Axel's forehead.

"Did she ever tell you what I did?"

"No, no sir, she didn't mention that." Axel's baritone pitched.

Mr. Mulls didn't blink. "I was an Interrogation Specialist. Did that job for fifteen years. Go on. You were saying."

Mrs. Mulls shook her head.

Wringing his sweaty hands, the explanation rushed from his mouth as if Mr. Mulls had threatened to short shackle him. "I was talking about Sara and the lawsuit that I had won. Apparently, Kerrigan was there and overheard that conversation. She must have thought I said those awful things about her. I understand how that conversation must have sounded and looked to her without knowing the full story, especially after our argument. What I don't understand is how she could think I'd ever say anything like that about her."

Mr. Mulls spoke, but only his lips moved. "Axel, why should I believe you?"

"Sir, I love your daughter. I wouldn't say or do anything to hurt her. I'm willing to do whatever is necessary to prove that to her."

"Dad, Axel's story checks out. I read articles about his ongoing legal troubles with Sara Murphy. I also had a buddy of mine, check Axel's story out." Jordan twisted his lips and avoided Axel's eyes.

"Why wouldn't she just confront you? Why did she quit her job and move? It seems this misunderstanding could have been resolved with a simple conversation," Mr. Mulls stated.

Axel raised his brow. "That's a great question. I wish I knew the answer."

"What did you argue about?" Mrs. Mulls asked.

"I wanted to take things to the next level. She didn't know, but I was going to propose to her the day of our argument. During our entire relationship, I've been the one pursuing her, and she's been running. Kerrigan wouldn't allow herself to believe that I loved her." He rubbed his chin. The memory of their argument haunted him. "She had a crazy idea that she wasn't good enough for me or that I'd want someone else. I became angry. I told her that I couldn't live with her constant expectations that I'd hurt her, and then I stormed out. My intention was to jar her, but my plan backfired in the worst possible way. Later that afternoon, Melody and I meet at the coffee shop. We were celebrating my victory, and that's when Kerrigan must have seen us." He closed his eyes, leaning back Axel rested his head against the sofa. "She left because she was heartbroken and that was all my fault."

Mr. Mulls unfolded his arms from across his chest. "And you're here to win her back?"

"Yes sir. I'm also here to ask your permission for her hand. I plan to win her back and never let her go again," Axel said confidently.

Mr. Mulls tilted his head, "What do you do for a living young man?"

"I own an advertising agency sir. Kerrigan worked for my company." Axel swallowed the lump in his throat.

Mr. Mulls' brow wrinkled. "And you love my daughter?"

"Yes. I've never felt about anyone the way I feel about Kerrigan. I want to spend the rest of my life with her."

Mr. Mulls glanced at Mrs. Mulls then back at Axel.

A wide grin spread from ear to ear, and she nodded her head. "Thank you for coming all this way for her, Axel. You seem to be a respectable young man. You have my blessing," Mrs. Mulls said.

Mr. Mulls inched to the edge of the recliner, elbows on his knees, hawk eyes zeroed in on Axel. "If you ever hurt my daughter, you better hope I don't find you."

Axel blinked twice. "Sir, I won't hurt her. I promise." He grabbed Mrs. Mulls, practically collapsing her lungs and then he shook Mr. Mulls' hand. "Sir, I love Kerrigan." His left hand swiped away perspiration from his brow. "Thank you both. I promise I only have the best intentions for your daughter. Thank you."

They talked a while longer. He told them about his parents and upbringing. He also told them about his company, how Kerrigan had been a stellar performer—one of the many things that drew him to her. At three o'clock, he and Jordan said their goodbyes. Jordan went back to his office. Axel headed back to the boutique and waited for Kerrigan's shift to end. With her parents' blessing, he was armed and ready to put his next steps into action.

***

At four thirty, Kerrigan's shift ended. She had a productive and busy day. The boutique had reached a new sales record and helping Sandy made her feel good. She also knew she would get a decent commission. With the baby on the way, she needed every dime she could make. She reached behind the counter grabbing the bag with the little blanket inside and her handbag. She made her way to where Sandy stood near the guest check out.

"Sandy, I'm leaving now. Thank you again for the gift. I love the blanket, and I appreciate your generosity."

"You're very welcome. After a day like this, I figure I still owe you." She smiled. "Oh, Kerrigan, don't forget your flowers. They're beautiful, and they were obviously sent out of love. You shouldn't let such a beautiful thing go to waste. Besides, the flowers will brighten your home." Sandy winked.

She stared at the arrangement again and swallowed hard. "You're right. They'll be lovely in my cottage. Thanks again. I'll see you tomorrow."

She took the vase and walked outside. Her arms were overloaded, but she only needed to make it to her car, parked at the other end of the lot. She walked down the sidewalk a few feet when she heard someone calling her name.

"Those flowers are almost as beautiful as you are. Can I help carry some of the load?"

The familiar voice echoed from behind, and her knees buckled as she spun around.

Before she hit the ground, strong arms enveloped Kerrigan. He brought her close to him, their bodies pressed firmly together as he gathered her up from the near collision with the hard concrete walkway.

She blinked rapidly, her eyes darting around her. She had never heard that pregnancy brain could cause hallucinations.

He led her to a nearby bench. Sandy rushed out and handed her a glass of water as Kerrigan slowly began to realize what was happening.

Axel kneeled down beside her, one of his hands holding hers. Face void of color and brows drawn, concern etched on his face. "You okay?" Axel asked.

"Axel?" she muttered, barely above a whisper. "What … why are you here?" she asked stammering, still stunned that she was looking at the man in the flesh and blood.

"I came for you, for us," he said, staring her up and down, and then studying her face. "After you're feeling better we need to talk. I'll wait for as long as it takes." He caressed her hand. "I'll be right back, sweetheart."

He stood and asked Sandy to step aside with him. Sandy frowned at the request, but joined him, never taking her eyes off Kerrigan. They spoke in hushed tones, and Kerrigan couldn't hear what was being said. There was no doubt that the flowers had come from Axel.

CHAPTER FIFTEEN

Axel held out his hand to help Kerrigan up from the bench. Nervous eyes stared at him. Seconds passed before she placed her hand in his and stood. He moved closer and placed his hand on the small of her back, the tingling feeling that started in his belly crawled up his spine. Escorting her to his silver rental car, he carried her bags, and she carried the bouquet. Once settled in the car, Axel searched her face intensely for a few moments, and then moved his eyes down her tiny frame. His gaze landed on the small belly bump. Eyes wide, his head jerked.

She faced the passenger window and inhaled a deep breath. Turning back to him she exhaled. "Axel, why are you here? Please don't do this to me." Tears flooded Kerrigan's eyes.

His tone was gentle. "I … I came here for you. I've been sick with worry." His eyes drawn to her mid-section again, fastened. "You shut me out, Kerrigan. You disappeared suddenly without a word. You wouldn't return my calls or emails. I needed to talk to you, and I knew the only way I could do that was to come to you. Since the day you left me, I've been miserable. What else was I supposed to do?"

He marveled at her belly again. Pulling the white sweater tightly around her waist, she tried to conceal her secret.

Axel drove toward the hotel neither saying a word. He cut a sidelong glance at her and she caught his eyes, turning away instantly. He cleared his throat every few minutes and she kept her attention on the world outside the passenger window, sighing occasionally.

They arrived fifteen minutes later. He hustled to the passenger side and helped her out the vehicle. Carrying her things, he led her through the lobby toward the elevators and up to his guest suite.

They walked inside his suite. She looked around, her eyes taking in the room's details, noted the baby grand piano and a large gift box seated on the bench. Fidgeting with nervous hands, she shifted from one foot to the next.

"That gift is for you," he said.

Her eyes stretched wide, and she nodded.

He closed and locked the door behind them, and then placed the bouquet and her bags on a foyer table. Without a word, he turned to face her, stepped forward and took her into his arms. Holding her tight against him, her baby bump pressed into his abdomen. He leaned down and covered her soft lips with his. Small hands placed on his chest trembled, and she clung to him, Axel's claim over Kerrigan hadn't been broken. After a few moments, he stopped and stared into her eyes. He took her by the hand and led her to a sofa that sat in front of a wall of glass doors overlooking San Diego Bay. When she was seated, he walked into the kitchen.

"I'll get us something to drink. Is lemonade okay?"

"Lemonade is fine," Kerrigan replied.

"Are you hungry? Can I get you something to eat?"

"No, thank you. I'm fine." Her voice trembled.

Restless hands wrung in her lap, and her eyes stayed fix to him, watched his every move as he poured two tall glasses of lemonade and swaggered leisurely back to the sofa. He placed both glasses down on the sofa table in front of them and then sat next to her so closely that their knees grazed.

He took both of her graceful hands into his masculine ones. "Is there something you need to tell me, sweetheart?" Axel asked, looking into her eyes, searching for the light that used to shine for him. A sudden pang struck him in the chest at the fear and sadness in her sunken eyes.

Kerrigan turned her face away.

He released the firm grip he had on one of her hands, covered her round belly with his large hand, long fingers gently massaging and caressing her through her dress. She flinched, but he steadied her by placing his other hand against the small of her back.

"When were you going to tell me?" he asked softly.

Kerrigan nodded her head. "I don't know," Kerrigan mumbled and looked down into her lap.

"Were you planning to keep our baby away from me?"

"Axel, I'm keeping the baby, and I don't expect or want anything from you. You'll never have to be burdened by the baby or me. I'll put this in writing if you want and then you can be on your merry way."

"Kerrigan, I'm hurt and surprised. You're pregnant, and you didn't plan to tell me. Why do you think I want nothing to do with you or our child? Our baby is the product of our love. After all of our lovemaking, everything we've shared, a baby was inevitable. My love for you has only gotten stronger. You're the only woman for me, the only woman I've ever wanted. You don't have to do this alone. We can raise our child together."

"Axel, you got what you wanted from me. I know you've moved on. Stop acting as though you care. What else do you want? Are you trying to hurt me deliberately?" She looked up at him, tears on the verge of spilling from her eyes like a waterfall.

"Baby, I haven't moved on. There isn't anyone else for me. It's only been you, always you. I've never lied to you, never betrayed you. I love you. There's been a huge misunderstanding. Please give me a chance to explain."

"You don't have to explain anything to me. What happened between us is in the past. I've accepted this fact, and I've moved on."

He moved closer to her, gently stroking her cheek as he gazed deeply into her, seeing her soul.

"Have you? Kerrigan, you're a terrible liar. The kiss we just shared says differently. Our baby growing inside you says differently. Your eyes say differently. Your heart says differently. I know what you think you saw and heard that day at the coffee shop. You only heard part of that conversation, and what you heard was out of context. I wish you had come to me and confronted me with what you thought. Just listen to me. I'm here to end the suffering for both of us, because Kerrigan, I've been lost without you. I'm hurting too. You broke my heart."

Glistening with moisture, her eyes widened—ready to erupt.

"The woman you saw me talking to is my cousin Melody. We were talking about Sara Murphy, the woman who tried to exhort money from my family and me. I've been in litigation with her for years, and I had just won my lawsuit against her." He searched her eyes. "Our conversation was about Sara and what you heard me saying was about her, not you, baby. I would never say such awful things about you. Do you know how badly I hurt knowing that you always think the worst of me? I'm a good man, Kerrigan. What can I do to prove myself to you?"

He thought back to the advice his father had given him.

"My father once told me that you get out of life what you expect, whether real or manufactured in your head. I didn't understand what he meant until you left me. You expected me to break your heart, and that's what you manufactured. You need to set different expectations of me, of us. I'm not the villain. I love you, and I expect to have a future with you."

***

Axel's handsome face contorted, and his eyes moistened. Kerrigan's mouth dropped open. His words registered clearly, and it all made sense. She hung her head, remaining silent for a few moments.

Tears streamed down Kerrigan's face, and she stuttered until the words leaped from her lips. "Axel, I, I don't know what to say. I ruined everything between us." She sobbed, gasping for air between words.

He lifted her chin and stared deeply into her eyes with his blue ones.

"Kerrigan, I love you. I need you. I want to work things out between us. That's why I'm here. What I want is for you to come home with me."

"How can you forgive me so easily? How can you want me back? I've ruined everything and treated you so unfairly. I was so stubborn."

"Love forgives. I was angry and stubborn. The way I stormed out on you that morning was cruel. When I discovered the reason you ran away, I was hurt, but my love for you is greater than any problem we could face. I've replayed my conversation with Melody repeatedly in my head. I understand how my words must have sounded, how she and I must have looked and how you must have felt. If I hadn't still been harboring such anger after all these years, I wouldn't have had that outburst, and none of this would have happened. I've spent the last couple of months in misery without you and I'm not leaving until you agree to come home with me."

Axel took her in his arms again and pulled her close.

"Axel, I'm sorry. I should have come to you before assuming and expecting the worst. I should have trusted you. I should have been honest with you about my feelings. I love you, Axel." The words rolled off Kerrigan's tongue easily. Trembling in his arms, her blurry eyes meet his eager gaze.

"I'm sorry, too. I shouldn't have been so harsh to you. I should have been patient. I love you, Kerrigan. I'll never stop loving you."

Taking her into his arms, he kissed her deeply, enrapturing her. She melted in his arms as she always did, wrapping her shaky fingers around the ridges of his muscular arms for her own strength.

He pulled away and spoke gently, but with authority now. "Baby, I'm not letting you go this time. I'm not letting you run away from our love, and I'm not slowing down. I want you, Kerrigan Mulls, and I will have you—this time on my terms. Do you understand my intentions for you?"

She nodded in agreement. Wrought with emotion, unable to speak and not fully comprehending the meaning of his words, she would do whatever he asked of her.

"Kerrigan, do you trust me?"

"Yes. I trust you."

"Kerrigan, I've missed you so much. I nearly lost my mind without you. Promise me that you'll never leave me again. Promise to come to me, to talk to me about anything, everything."

"Axel, I'm so sorry for hurting you. I promise not to leave you again. We'll work through our problems together. I love you."

He wrapped her in his arms and held her close in silence for a long while as they took in the view of the bay.

***

Axel was soft and gentle with her. He lifted her from the sofa and carried her to the bedroom. Slowly, sensually he slipped her arms out of the straps, freeing her of the dress she wore. He laid her down on the bed and kissed her tenderly, starting at her thighs and trailing his lips up to her stomach, between her bosoms and then capturing her bottom lip. Her body shivered at the touch of his hands.

"Ah. Axel," she moaned softly.

Swiftly, he rose and ripped his white shirt away from his flesh. After yanking down his jeans and gray boxer briefs, she gasped at his naked body, and a fully erected cock. Kneeling between her quivering thighs, he spread her wide and eased into her haven. "I love you, I need you. I can't live without you," he whispered into her ear.

Breathless, she whimpered back, "I love you. I need you. I'm sorry."

"Shh. Enough of sorry. Feel how much I love you, Kerrigan."

Waves crashed against the shoreline in sync with his deep thrusts. Their bodies united unlike any other time before, more spiritual, sensual and emotional. This time when they made love, their souls mated.

"Axel. Ah. Axel."

Deep thrusts measured with purpose, he took his time, whispering softly. "Oh, Kerrigan. I love you. I love you."

The pillow soaked with tears, his mixed with hers.

"Axel, I … I," she stammered, sensation and feeling flowing through her stifled her words.

Freed, she gave her mind, body and heart to him, completely unrestrained. "Axel, I don't want to live without you," she cried out in rapture.

The union was like the first time they had discovered each other.

Merging into her, his tempo was steady. "You never will," he panted heavily.

In the afterglow of their encounter, he held her tightly against his drenched body as she lay on top of him.

"Kerrigan, can I ask you a question?"

She rose, propping herself up on his chest and looking into his eyes. "Yes," she said softly.

"Do you know why I love you?"

She gazed down at him. "No, I really don't."

He searched her eyes. "Well, you have a beautiful spirit. You always put others ahead of yourself. You're the first woman I've ever met who hasn't asked me for a dime, and instead have given me something more than all the money in the world—your heart and your capacity for love, not superficial lust. You have a brilliant mind, and I admire your hard work and independence."

Still staring into her eyes, he stroked her cheek softly. "I was a broken man after the ordeal with Sara. I was afraid to trust and filled with anger. For years, I surrounded myself with empty shallow women. Women I knew I couldn't get close to, and I was lonely. When you walked into my office, I was forced to open my eyes. I don't know how, but I knew—I loved you from the start."

His face went blurry, and her chest heaved, unable to catch her breath. "I thought you were like all the other men I dated in the past, and there weren't very many, but they all treated me the same. They told me I was pretty, but in the end, they only wanted one thing. None of them respected my mind, and when I refused to give them my body ..."

She paused, the dam behind her eyes bursting as tears streamed down her cheeks. "I expected to be treated that way, I expected to be rejected and hurt. My insecurities have nothing to do with you or our differences. They have to do with me believing that the only thing a man could be interested in, was my body. With you, it's different. The way you look at me, the things you say and do. I had no choice but to love you."

He tightened his grip on her and lifted his head to kiss her softly. "Our souls recognized what neither of us knew—we are the completion of each other. We are bound by love."

She couldn't hold back any longer. Tears flowed down Kerrigan's cheeks, and he swiped them away. They lie there entwined and fully sated. For the first time in months, she slept soundly in Axel's arms.

***

Saturday, January 5

Light streaming into the room forced his eyelids open. He reached out for her, but instead, his hand glided over the smooth, cool bed sheet. He stretched his arms out, a wide grin extended from one ear to the other. He would have felt a twinge of panic, but things between them were changed forever. After the night they shared, she wouldn't leave him again. They had talked all night long, coming to terms with their love and putting aside their insecurities and fears.

He lay there content for a few minutes before a heavenly aroma wafted in from the kitchen. His stomach growled. Part one of his plan had worked exactly as he had hoped—get the girl back. Now for part two of his plan—keep the girl. He picked up his phone and dialed.

Axel swaggered lazily into the kitchen. Kerrigan scooped a spoonful of eggs onto a plate piled high with pancakes. He walked up behind her and wrapped her in the warm embrace of his arms spanning her waist, caressing her belly.

He kissed the side of her neck. "Good morning beautiful. How are you feeling?"

She spun around, the long white flowing dress that he bought for her fanning out, and wrapped her arms around his neck. *God, she's beautiful!*

"I've never felt better. What about you?" Returning to her task of preparing breakfast for them, she glided to the refrigerator, floating. He loved that he did that to her.

"Baby, I feel the same as you." He smiled, leaned down and gently kissed her plump lips.

He pulled away, his brow furrowed in deep thought. "When is our baby due?"

"July 17."

"Good. There's time."

"Time for what?" she asked curiously.

"I have a surprise that I want you to enjoy before the baby gets here. Now what are you cooking in here, besides that bun in the oven?"

She giggled. "I made pancakes, eggs and bacon."

He closed his eyes, inhaling. “Hmm. Let’s eat. We have places to go today.”

“Where are we going?”

“I’m not telling.”

CHAPTER SIXTEEN

Kerrigan leaned forward, her head turning right and then left as she peered through the passenger and driver's side windows. She recognized the route he took.

"McBride is this close to signing with us," he said mimicking the space of an inch between his index finger and thumb. This topic would distract her curiosity.

"That's great! What happens next? Do I still get to work on the account? At least until…" she said looking down at her belly.

"Yes, of course. That's completely up to you. I got the call a couple of weeks ago. We have a meeting with him to go over the finer details two weeks from now. Your brilliance, your creativity is what landed McBride." He gleamed. At last, she was his again. "You know, after the baby gets here, you could always open the boutique you've always wanted."

"I don't have the start-up capital. Besides, no bank worth doing business with is going to give me the size loan I'd need to get started."

He flexed his brow up and down. "You don't happen to know any wealthy investors who might be willing to give you the working capital you'd need, do you?" He smirked.

"I'd never ask to borrow that kind of money from you!"

"I'd never *let* you borrow that kind of money from me, I'd give it to you. You don't get a say in this," he said, his tone decidedly decisive. "I believe you can do anything you set your mind to."

She pierced him with her round eyes and spoke her thoughts. "You always get what you want, don't you?"

He reached out and squeezed her knee. "I do." She squirmed at the tickle of his touch. "You should know that by now," he said, one corner of his mouth slanting up.

The car rounded the corner, and then slowed to a crawl. She whipped her head around and pinned him with a puzzled look.

"It's okay, baby. Jordan won't kill me. How do you think I found you?"

He told her the whole story of how he had hired a private investigator to find her, contacted Jordan and gained his trust. Her red cheeks glowed.

"You both must think I'm such a ridiculous and silly woman," she replied.

"No. You and I each played our part. Let's not dwell on the past anymore. We're moving forward together. We're here so I can meet your family properly. I also need to help you pack up your things from the cottage."

"You know about the cottage too? Wow, you must have hit it off with Jordan."

"I think so. He and I speak the same language."

"Did he tell you about the baby?" she asked.

"No. He didn't share that news with me." He placed his hand under her chin. "Come on, sweetheart. Quit the stalling. It's time to go inside."

***

He took her hand and held it tightly. Her shoes tapped against the hard concrete path as they walked to the house. She unlocked the front door, and they walked inside, pausing at the entrance of the family room. Her eyes scanned the room. To her surprise, everyone was there. Jordan, Nicole and their daughters, her mom and dad, his parents, Aunt Emma, Ryker and Ashley were all there. As she registered each person's face, tears welled behind her eyes. Her hand flew up to cover her mouth, and she staggered, grabbing Axel's arm to keep her balance.

He wrapped his arms around her waist, caressing her belly, and then leaned down to her ear. "It's okay, baby. They're all here to celebrate with us. Jordan explained everything to your parents. I explained everything to mine. Everyone knows about the baby too," he whispered.

The dam inside her broke as tears spilled down her cheeks. She turned in his arms and stared up into his eyes, lips trembling, speechless.

He kissed her softly on the forehead. "Come on, everyone's watching. Let's go say hello." Breaking his hold, he stepped forward, turned slightly and held out his hand. Kerrigan's grasp was so firm, her nails digging into his flesh formed small crescents in his palms.

Axel led Kerrigan to her mother and father, who stood next to built-in bookcases at the other end of the family room.

Her mother pulled Kerrigan into a hug. "I'm so glad you worked out your problems. He seems like a wonderful young man."

"He is wonderful." A lovesick grin eclipsed her face.

Stepping forward, her father held her at arm's length, studying her. Creases formed at the edge of his lips into a smile. "You look happy, sweet pea."

"I am happy daddy." She beamed.

He wrapped her in his protective hold and whispered in her ear. "Axel better treat you right and if he doesn't…"

She interrupted her father's lecture. "He will. This was my fault, not Axel's. He's a great man."

Her father released her and turned to Axel.

"Good to see you again young man," Mr. Mulls said.

"Good you see you again, too, sir," Axel replied.

Kerrigan frowned and looked at him. "Again?" She whispered.

"I'll tell you later." He winked at her.

Kerrigan's father gripped his chin. "I can see that you love my daughter. Whoever makes my baby girl happy makes me happy too."

Axel pulled Kerrigan into his side, grabbing her around her waist. "Yes, I love Kerrigan very much. She means the world to me."

She rested her head on his chest, addressing her parents. "I love Axel, too."

"I'm so glad you two were able to straighten out your misunderstanding," Mrs. Mulls said.

"Me too," Axel said, tightening his grip around Kerrigan.

Mrs. Mulls touched Axel gently on the shoulder. "Jordan told me you lost a business deal just to be here."

Kerrigan jerked her head up and caught his eyes. "What! Axel, you didn't tell me that. I, I'm sorry. I didn't realize." She apologized.

He leaned down. "You're worth much more than a business deal." He flashed a grin and then whispered to her. "Besides, you'll have all the time in the world to make it up to me." His attention turned back to Mr. and Mrs. Mulls. "If you'll please excuse me, I'd like to say hello to Jordan."

Walking pass a side table filled with family pictures, Axel sauntered toward Jordan and Nicole. Reaching his hand out, Axel shook Jordan's hand. "Jordan, I can't thank you enough for all of your help and support."

"I'm glad I was a part of your reunion. You and I are going to be good friends."

"I have no doubt," Axel said.

Wrapping their manly arms around each other careful not to get too close, they gave each other the standard man hug.

Next, they greeted Axel's parents.

"Kerrigan, you look perfectly radiant. I'm so excited about being a grandmother. I've enjoyed meeting your lovely family." Mrs. Christensen gave Kerrigan a hug.

"You've done well. You took my advice," Axel's father said as he shook Axel's hand. "You've created one heck of a moment."

Emma gave each of them a squeeze. "Kerrigan, you're beautiful as always. I knew you would find your way back to each other."

"Thank you Emma," she said.

They made their way to Ashley and Ryker. The pair was deep in conversation and stood away from the group near a window overlooking the perfectly landscaped garden. Ashley's face lit up like stars in the evening desert sky.

Her mouth dropped open when she saw Kerrigan's round tummy. "Kerri! Oh. My. God. You're glowing. You look adorable. We have a lot of catching up to do." Ashley placed her hand on Kerri's belly. "I should have known he knocked you up. Axel could never keep his hands off you. Obviously it wasn't only his hands that he had a problem keeping to himself." Ashley laughed.

"Ash!" She giggled and rolled her eyes at her friend. "I've missed you and your scandalous tongue so much."

Finally, they greeted Ryker. "Axel and Kerrigan, I'm happy for you both. Bro, I'm glad you finally pulled your head out of your..."

Axel interrupted his brother. "Ryker, me too," he replied.

***

Everyone mingled and chatted before Nicole announced that a buffet-style lunch was ready. Axel made a plate for Kerrigan.

"Sweetheart, you need to eat. Then I want you to take me to the cottage. I want to see what all needs to be moved." He leaned in close so that only she could hear. "And I want to be alone with you for a while. I'll sneak out ahead of you so that we're unnoticed. Meet me there in ten minutes."

She slipped Axel the key. "Okay, in ten minutes."

***

Axel walked to the cottage behind the house at the far end of the multi-acre backyard. The cottage was fenced in, set against the backdrop of looming mountains. He made his way down the winding, descending path that led to the front door. The key inserted into the knob, he unlocked the door and stepped inside, waiting.

Ten minutes later, the front door screeched opened. He stood at the other end of the small room, leaning against the kitchen bar, his gaze caressing Kerrigan as she glided pass the threshold.

"The space is cozy and nicely decorated. Don't you think?" she asked.

"Uh, huh." The last thing on his mind was the coziness or decor of the cottage. "Is the front door locked?" he asked.

"Yes. Why?"

Tempting eyes bore into her soul. "You know why."

He stalked toward her, pinned her against the living room wall, and then whispered hoarsely in her ear. "I don't want us to be disturbed."

Without pause or hesitation, his lips captured hers, his hard bulge pressed into her stomach. Impatient hands slid down Kerrigan's bosom to her thighs. He quickly lifted her dress and massaged her thighs as he parted them en route to his destination. His fingers dipped into the side of her panties and dug into her folds. Liquid heat awaited his touch.

***

She writhed and moaned at his stroke. He anchored his hand against the wall, raised her leg high and placed it in the crook of his arm, holding her steady in this position. His fingers went to work. He inserted one, then another and finally a third finger, pumping into her core.

"You like this, Kerrigan?"

"Yes," she muttered breathlessly.

He continued fingering her, stroking inside her until she climaxed. He lowered his arm, carefully bringing her leg down.

"I'm not done with you yet, sweetheart. I want you out of your mind."

She moaned, and her eyes rolled back. "Oh, yes."

He slithered down her body and planted his knees on the hardwood. In slow motion, he guided her panties to the ground, cuffing her ankles. One foot at a time, she stepped out of the thongs and kicked them across the floor. He lifted her leg again and placed her bare foot onto his shoulder. Axel dove into her haven with his tongue, delighting in her sweet, succulent taste.

"You taste good. I love how sweet you are." He groaned.

"Ah, Axel."

He French kissed her sex, sliding his tongue pass her slick, delicate folds and plunging deep into her moist center. She trembled, her legs weak under his sexual barrage.

Soft breaths formed into words barely spoken. "Feels so good." She whispered.

He continued his work, enjoying her wet treasure until she climaxed again.

She cried out loudly. "Oh Axel, you're amazing."

"Baby, I'm still not done with you. I want more."

***

Axel lowered her leg down from his shoulder and then he stood. His cock at full attention and ready to drive into her hard.

Taking her hand, he led her up the stairs to the loft bedroom. He guided her to the bed. Nimble hands raised Kerrigan's dress over her head. She wore only her periwinkle lacy bra and her Brazilian wax. Axel leaned behind her and unfastened her bra, her plump caramel breasts released. Eager hands unbuttoned and removed his shirt, exposing his muscles rippled beneath. Kerrigan watched him greedily. In one swift motion, he yanked off his jeans and boxer briefs, freeing his erection. Her round eyes enlarged, and a quiet gasp escaped her lips.

***

She lowered herself to her knees and took him into her hands. Axel stilled. Kerrigan marveled at the feel of him, her hands sliding up and down his long thick shaft. His thick member pulsed in small hands barely able to wrap around his girth. Slowly, she lowered her mouth onto his mushroom tip, swirling her tongue in a circular motion and then took him deep into her throat. Ingesting him, the pad of her tongue stroked his hard cock.

"Oh, baby!" He groaned.

She sucked and stroked his cock until he lifted her up from bent knees.

They stood, naked bodies pressed firmly together, breathless. He enveloped her in his strong arms and devoured her with his kiss, the sensual heat between them wild and untamable. They tumbled onto the bed, her body trapped beneath his. He sucked on her peaked nipples as he spread her legs widely apart and lifted them over his shoulders. He plunged his cock deep inside her, stretching her to accommodate his size.

Filled and overwhelmed with his cock inside her, she cried out. "Ah. Ah."

The mattress squealed and the headboard banged against the wall in synchronized harmony with his thrusts. Enraptured, her legs quaked with tremors and the room began to spin around her.

In repeated motion, he raised his hips high, nearly pulling himself out of her, before slamming into her once more. He quickened the pace of his thrusts. She whimpered and moaned loudly and pushed back against each of Axel's blows. The pleasure inside her so intense, her body quaked as he continued plowing into her. Axel pinned her hands above her head and muffled her screams with his deep kisses. Her walls clenched around his rigid cock, every nerve ending fired simultaneously. The sensation pulsed through her, started at her core and moved in waves, and then rippled through every inch of her body.

She screamed out his name. "Axel. Oh. Axel. Axel."

***

Driving into her fast and deep, Axel raised up on his knees giving him a full view of his cock slamming into her, their contrasting flesh tones merged into one. Kerrigan's loud screams his aphrodisiac, he hammered into her until she silenced from exhaustion. He rammed his cock into her over, and over again until at last, he found his release. He exploded deep into her, pushing her over the edge. She gripped his arms, digging into his flesh. Her entire body convulsed as she screamed his name again.

Still buried deep inside her, he leaned down and kissed her deeply. "I love you so much, baby," he said with panted breath.

"I love you too." She returned breathlessly. "I've loved you for a long time."

He caressed her cheek with his knuckles. "I know, baby," he said with a gentle smile.

***

Kerrigan reminisced about their relationship over the past year and everything that had transpired between them to this point. She was finally able to express her unbridled love for Axel freely and willingly. Tears of joy burned behind her eyes as she poured out her soul to him.

"Axel, I was afraid to love you, afraid to lose you, afraid to get lost in you. No matter the cost, I want you to know how I feel, how much you mean to me. You're everything to me. You're thoughtful, caring, loving and tender. You make me feel safe. You make me laugh. You make me smile. You make me cry. You make me feel whole." Kerrigan's eyes heavy with tears, he held her firmly in his arms. "I could go on for days about your body, and how hot you make me. You have me heart, mind, body and soul. I'm not afraid to admit that I want more than a sexual fling with you. I love you. With everything in me, I love you Axel." Tears burst from her eyes and washed her face.

He stared tenderly into her wet orbs. "Kerrigan, I know you love me. I've known for a while, but to hear you say the words, to express your love for me in that way makes me the happiest man in the world. I never want you to be afraid to love me. Your love is safe with me. Your heart is home with me." They embraced each other tightly. She never wanted to let go.

***

After basking in the afterglow of their passion and confessions of love, they dressed, realizing that their absence from the main house would be recognized by now.

Sitting on the bed, he put on his shoes. "Baby, sit here with me for a minute." He smoothed out the spot next to him. "There's something we need to work out before we head back inside. Can we talk?" he asked, his tenor and countenance sobering.

Snapped out of her euphoric state, "What's wrong?" She asked with tremors clinging to the end of her words.

Her voice pitched, and she arched her brow, anchored beside him as her fingers curled around the edge of the mattress, clawing the floral comforter.

Axel watched her beautiful flustered face contort, and the corners of his lips curled upward. "Baby, you know I love everything about you, right?" He paused, and then covered her hand resting on the mattress with his. "You're beautiful, incredibly intelligent, talented, kind and sexy…"

"But? What's wrong, Axel? Please tell me," she pleaded.

"…but, your name bugs the hell out of me."

She narrowed her eyes at him, as though he had grown three heads and was speaking some alien dialect. "You can call me by my nickname, Kerri or…"

Axel interrupted before she could finish. "Oh no, sweetheart, that's not what I mean." He gazed at her with lips drawn into a straight line. "It's not your first name that I take issue with."

Kerrigan frowned. "I, I don't understand."

"Your last name is all wrong. What are we going to do about that Miss Mulls?"

With this, he smiled deviously, leaned toward the nightstand and opened the top drawer pulling out the tiny white box he had placed there before she arrived. He opened the box and shaky fingers lifted out the custom platinum, four-carat diamond princess cut ring.

Her eyes turned to oceans and she cupped her mouth with mouth hands, gasping for air.

Axel dropped to his knees, burrowing into the pile of thick gray carpet. "Your last name should be Christensen." Taking her left hand, he slid the ring onto her finger.

Tears spilled down her cheeks in waterfalls.

"Kerrigan, I want you, forever. Will you take my last name? Will you commit your mind, heart, body and soul to me for life? Will you marry me?"

***

Kerrigan's chest heaving, she tried to speak, but her words were paralyzed in her throat. This had to be a dream. He couldn't be real.

"After how badly I've treated you? I … I'm ... " she stammered incoherently, unable to find the right words. She took a deep breath and started again. "Axel, you really want to marry me? Not because I'm pregnant, right?"

He rolled his eyes and shook his head. "No, not because you're pregnant," he said softly, running the pad of his thumb under her tear-stained eyes. "Kerrigan, I've wanted you since the first day I met you, and I've been in love with you as long. The baby has nothing to do with me wanting to marry you. Of course, your having our first child does give us an incentive to move things along faster. He or she already takes after me."

She beamed, closing her teary eyes. "I didn't imagine this in a million years."

"We can be married in a month before you're actually showing."

"You do move fast! I don't know what to say."

"This is where you say 'yes'," he said, his tone playfully stern.

She leaned down, her fingers tangling his thick hair. "Yes! Yes, I'll marry you! I love you, Axel."

"I love you too, baby." He gave her a grin that nearly split his face in two.

***

After their romp in the cottage, they returned to the main house an hour and a half later. Entering through the kitchen's French doors with steps as light as feathers, they sneaked their way into the family room where everyone was still gathered.

Huddled on leather loungers with Ashley in an unlit corner as Axel and Kerrigan tiptoed pass, Ryker cleared his throat. Kerrigan gasped, and Axel jerked back.

"Where have you two been?" Ryker asked, not looking up from his smart phone as busy fingers swiped across the screen.

"We had some unfinished business to take care of," Axel replied. "Speaking of unfinished business, can I get everyone's attention? I have an announcement to make." Continuing his journey, he stepped into the center of the gathering.

The room stilled, every voice hushed, every movement ceased and every eye riveted to Axel, Kerrigan at his side.

"First, I want to thank you all for coming today. Jordan and Nicole, I appreciate everything you've done to open your home to my family and me. I can't thank you enough. As you all know, Kerrigan and I are expecting the arrival of our first child in July next year. We're both extremely excited and can't wait to meet our new son or daughter. However, we hope you'll join us for one more celebration." He reached for Kerrigan's hand and looked deeply into her eyes. "Kerrigan has just accepted my hand in marriage. We'll be married in a month, and I'm the happiest man in the world. Thank you, Mr. and Mrs. Mulls, for your blessing." He looked over and winked at Kerrigan.

"My family knows this, and so does Kerrigan, but I want to share with everyone in the room, my new family." He glanced around at the faces in the room before steadying his gaze on her. Continuing, he looked deeply into her eyes. "I knew the day that I met you that I loved you. I wanted to drop to my knees and ask you to marry me then, but I think you would have slapped me. When you left my office, I immediately called dad and told him that I had met the woman who would turn my world right side up, and you did. Thank you for giving me a chance, and for allowing me to love you, sweetheart. You rescued a lonely soul and made him whole."

***

Family and friends crowded around them. Kerrigan stared longingly into his eyes. He leaned down and kissed her passionately.

The women in the room giggled and swooned, then everyone clapped.

"Axel, where are you going for your honeymoon?" Jordan asked.

A wide grin saddled his face. "I want Kerrigan to enjoy being my bride, and I plan to pamper her until the baby arrives. We'll be taking multiple trips. Our first stop is Denver. It's a breathtaking place this time of the year, and it's my special gift to Kerrigan since I told her that I'd take her there someday. We'll be there an entire month." He winked at her.

***

Axel cornered Kerrigan as she leaned against the navy and white striped paper-covered wall in a quiet spot just outside of the family room and away from the others.

"You seem distant. Is everything okay, sweetheart?" Axel's eyes searched hers.

Butterflies swarmed her stomach in his presence. She thought about the first step she had taken to change her life, the step into his office for the interview. She smiled. Laura Stephens was right—all it took was the first step and everything else fell into place. She was blissfully elated with life and love, and Axel.

She placed her hands against his rigid chest and looked up into his eyes. "Everything is perfect. I'm still in shock. I didn't recognize your love when it was right there in front of me, and I almost let this go," she said gesturing between them with her hand. "I don't deserve you."

He wrapped his hulking arms tightly around her waist, pulled her close and whispered into her ear. "Kerrigan, it's the other way around. Someone like me doesn't deserve a woman as sexy, beautiful, intelligent and as kind as you are. I'm looking forward to spending the rest of my life loving you and giving you the world. Sweetheart, I love you with all my heart, and I can't wait to show you how much, over and over, again." He pulled away and flashed his sinister grin.

She blushed and leaned helplessly into him. She had found her Mr. Right. "I love you so much. I've waited so long for you. Thank you."

He frowned. "For?"

"For loving me enough to wait for me, despite myself," she said.

He shrugged his shoulders. "Hmm, did I have a choice?" he teased.

"You always have a choice," she said.

He leaned down and cupped her face between his large hands. His tender kisses landed on her forehead, then nose and then lips, lingering until she went limp in his arms. "Baby, that's where you're wrong, I never stood a chance. Loving you is the only choice." He pulled her closer. "I'm never letting go."

The story continues in book three, Take Me Down.

Excerpt from Take Me Down

***

CHAPTER ONE

"It's not what you think Ash. Hear me out babe. She doesn't mean anything to me. I screwed up." Paul groveled on his rusty knees, kneeling near the bedside as Ashley shoved pass him. "I was vulnerable and weak. Babe, please don't do this. I promise I won't mess up again."

Ashley whipped her head around and shot fiery daggers at Paul with her eyes. "The sad thing is that you don't even care, and that's a problem for me. I'm tired of your bullshit. I won't do this with you anymore. We're done. Get out!"

Paul crawled across the floor and covered his bare pasty ass crack with the crumpled sheet as he wrapped his lower half. The rail thin skank, whom he was screwing senselessly when Ashley walked into the room, crouched naked in a corner scrambling to dress. Arms and legs flailed wildly as the skinny red haired woman shoved her freckled face through the neck hole of her pink shirt and yanked up a pale gray skirt around her absent hips. Scrambling, she grabbed her checkered Mary Jane pumps, leopard print bra and panties and made her shameful escape through the front door of the loft apartment.

Finally, on his feet, Paul stalked over to Ashley and snaked his sweat-drenched biceps around her waist and pulled her to him. "Ashley, you know this is your fault. If you didn't hold out on me last week, I wouldn't have …"

She jerked out of his grimy grip and spun around. With the full force of breath in her lungs, Ashley's scream bounced off the twenty-foot ceiling. "Get your goddamn hands off me! How dare you blame me, you piece of *shit*! Get out! Now!" Trembling hands clenched into fists. "Get your shit and get the hell out."

Paul stilled. He backed away. Kept quiet. A smirk smeared across his face, he meandered across the room in his boxers and leaned against the speckled granite kitchen countertop. "Ash, come on. I swear. I'll never cheat on you again."

A coy smile relaxed the tension in her lips. "Last time, huh?" Her stare idled on perfect bleach-white teeth that he dared to bare.

"I swear. This is the last time. You're my beautiful mocha princess."

Moving at a snail's pace, she retrieved his black slacks and dress shirt that were tossed carelessly to the floor near shiny new loafers. She slinked pass him and wiggled her voluptuous ass. With a slight turn and a flippant tilt of her head, she glanced over her shoulder. "You're right, damn asshole." She tossed his belongings through the large industrial window nine stories to the ground below. "I said get out, and that's what I meant. Now!"

Suddenly, Ashley lunged forward, her clawed hands aimed at his jugular. Stumbling, he crashed into a leather stool and landed on the cold concrete floor.

Paul scrambled to his feet. Backing away from Ashley, he slammed into the gritty brick wall. "You crazy bitch."

"I'll show you crazy." She stepped out of her shoes, bent down and retrieved a four-inch stiletto, heel aimed at Paul.

The brick grated his flesh as he slithered along the wall's surface trying to escape. Ashley charged again. Paul scurried to the front door. His sweaty hand fiddled with the knob, and he made his escape.

Paul stood half-naked in the hall. The door slammed shut. Ashley laughed, thinking about him running through the interior of the building in his boxers. He hadn't been wise to tempt her sanity.

With Paul evicted from her apartment and her life, Ashley sunk to the floor. She pulled her knees up to her chest and lowered her head into them. Her anger burned hot, she'd forgotten to breath. Stewing in her reality, she sobbed hard as tears flowed in streams down her face like a waterfall.

Ashley and Paul had met at a bar. That first night of heated passion had been a deceptive lure. The explosive sex that started with midnight booty calls quickly fizzled into a year of pure hell. Paul came equipped with a heartbeat and a hard cock, barely a step up from dildo sex. They had nothing in common, he was rude and frankly, the man was dumber than the loafers that hit pavement when she tossed them out the window. He just happened to have the right male apparatus to soothe the empty ache between her thighs on lonely nights. She turned to men whenever the solace in her life was too overwhelming, echoed too loudly and reminded her that fairytale endings didn't always happen, though her best friend Kerrigan proved to be the exception. *Bitch.*

After her pity party, Ashley reveled in a sense of relief. The thought of that bargain basement hooker in her apartment having sex on her bed made Ashley's stomach twist. She pulled herself up from the floor. With puffy eyes, she entered the bathroom to clean up, dabbed tears away from her swollen brown orbs.

Returning to the loft's main living area, she slid on a pair of flip-flops and exited. The elevator ride down to the apartment's main lobby didn't take long. Waving to Carl, the door attendant who she always caught sleeping on the job, she pushed the doors open and walked out. Ashley pressed the talk button on her hands-free earpiece.

"Hello," the winded husky male voice belted out.

"Hey, Axel, this is Ash. Is Kerri home?"

"Hi." He paused. "Uh, yeah. Hold on a minute." His annoyed tone didn't faze her.

Ashley's Yorkie circled brightly lit lampposts and yipped at strangers strolling down the dark sidewalk in front of her apartment building. She tugged Copper's leash, attempting to keep him from biting and yelping at passersby.

A small breathless voice whispered in her ear. "Hey Ash. You never call this late. What's going on? Are you okay?"

Kerrigan didn't sound like herself. "Kerri, did I catch you at a bad time?" Ashley's eyes stretched wide, and her jaw dropped. "Oh. God. You and Axel aren't fu ..." Ashley halted her words as she caught the crumpled frown of a craggy old woman who resembled a character from a Mother Goose Nursery Rhyme. "Oh. God. You are screwing." She stared brazenly at the old hag and rolled her eyes. "I'm sorry I called after ten. I forgot married people with a baby only have sex at night. Can I call you tomorrow?"

Kerrigan let out a guilty giggle. "Ash! You know I'm always here for you. Let's talk now. What's wrong?" Ashley heard Axel grumbling in the background.

"Kerri, go take care of your man. Axel is still my boss. You don't have to deal with him since you're off running your boutique. I don't need your grumpy husband after me on Monday."

Kerrigan laughed again. "Don't worry about Axel. I've already taken care of him. We can talk now. Do you want me to come over?"

Ashley let out a sigh, and tears pooled in her eyes. "Oh, Kerri. I love you. My life is a mess and, and, I … Shit!"

In a rush of frenzy, she bolted down the sidewalk, her legs carrying her as fast as she could move them. "Copper come back! No, no! Oh my God. No! Copper!" Ashley's cell phone crashed to the ground, the face of her smart phone shattered into hundreds of pieces on the concrete.

Out of breath, tears leaked a trail across her cheeks, and tangled hair whipped across her face, Ashley surrendered to the full force of her emotions. If anyone deserved to have a mental breakdown at ten thirty on a Wednesday night in the middle of Peachtree Street, she did. Pacing up and down the block, she took rapid steps and muttered under her breath. Attempting to skirt a man who jogged pass her, their shoulders grazed, and she nearly fell.

Ashley lost it. "Excuse you, asshole." She trailed behind the man, quickening her gait to a stride. His legs carried him full sprint. Her pursuit halted at the end of the block as the crosswalk signal changed. Two lanes of idling cars were the great divide between Ashley and her assailant.

Yelling from the opposite side of the road with confidence, "lunatic," he turned and continued on his way.

Her heart pounded in her chest. She glared at the man's back getting smaller and smaller until he disappeared into the night. Breathless, she limped back to the front of her building and leaned over, open palms pressed against her knees.

Two minutes later, her shallow breathing returned to normal and she stood up. Ashley moved her hand to her tear-stained face and wiped the moisture away. Suddenly, a warm sensation blanketed her right shoulder.

Ashley jumped. "Ah!" She whirled around. "You can't rob someone on one of the shittiest days of their life! I don't have any damn money."

The stranger snatched his masculine hand away and stepped back. Slowly, her eyes settled on his Nike sneakers, crawled up his navy jogging pants to a muscular chest and then landed on a face so perfect that she had to lift up her jaw up from the sidewalk.

"Miss, I'm not going to hurt you. Are you okay?" The handsome stranger's voice soothed her fear.

She stared into his gray eyes. The man was gorgeous. "Yes, I'm okay. I've just had a bad day. Thanks."

About Lauren H. Kelley

Lauren began writing short stories in high school, but abandoned her first love to pursue a business degree and career in corporate America. A late bloomer to her true calling and craft, she finally figured out what she wanted to do with her life—write! Growing up in a multicultural family, she was exposed to diversity from an early age. She has always had an appreciation and respect for multicultural romance and aims to bridge the racial divide through her novels and short stories. She currently resides in the Southeast.

Visit laurenhkelley.com for other titles in the
Suits in Pursuit series.

Pull Me Closer (book one)
Take Me Down (book three is coming in 2014)

Find Lauren H. Kelley on:
Laurenhkelley.com
Facebook.com/authorlaurenhkelley
Twitter: @laurenhkelley

CPSIA information can be obtained at www.ICGtesting.com
Printed in the USA
LVOW04s1840060715

445142LV00027B/589/P